INNOCENT BYSTANDERS

Following her own warning against looking, Martha had seen nothing of the nearby confrontation that broke out between the four men. She and Ed had nearly passed the lot, and she'd almost managed to put the men out of her mind, when she heard two short, flat, loud pops.

"Ed!" she gasped, turning. "What was that?"

"Gunshots!" Ed answered. He, too, turned to see what was happening.

They saw two of the men down. A third was running straight for them.

"Oh, my God, Ed, he's coming after us!" Martha shouted, taking a step back on the sidewalk.

Ed wasn't worried about the fleeing man. He was more concerned with the fact that the fourth man had a gun raised as if about to shoot, and if he did, he and Martha would be in the line of fire.

"Martha, get down!" He grabbed his wife reflexively and pulled her down to the sidewalk with him. . .

LAW & ORDER

IN DEEP

A novel by Jack Gregory
based on the Universal television series
LAW AND ORDER
created by
Dick Wolf

ST. MARTIN'S PAPERBACKS

Published by arrangement with MCA Publishing Rights, a Division of MCA Inc.

LAW AND ORDER: IN DEEP

Copyright © 1993 by MCA Publishing Rights, a Division of MCA Inc.

Front cover photograph courtesy The Stock Market.

ISBN: 0-312-95007-1

Printed in the United States of America

St. Martin's Paperbacks edition/February 1993

10 9 8 7 6 5 4 3 2 1

Chapter One

A taxi driver, impatient at the pace of traffic on Fifty-seventh Street, pulled out from behind a bus and accelerated quickly. At the last moment a middle-aged couple stepped off the curb in front of him. The driver hit the horn and stood on his brakes, squalling to a stop. The middle-aged couple, who had waited patiently for the "Walk" light, continued across the street as if the driver wasn't even there.

"Where the hell you from, mister? Ain't you ever seen a car before?" the taxi driver shouted in frustration. Because he had to brake to avoid them, he had no choice now but to get back in line behind the bus and wait for the light to

3

change. The couple, oblivious to the taxi driver's frustration, continued to walk back toward their hotel.

The man was in his mid- to late fifties, average-sized, with gray hair and beard. The woman was a little younger, with hair that still clung to its original dark color. She was carrying a bag from one of the pricey little shops in Trump Towers. She nudged her husband to point out two black men who were standing near a Dumpster in the parking lot alongside the Executive Stress Athletic Club.

"Ed," she whispered apprehensively, "do you see those two men standing over there?"

"What men?"

"Those black men," the woman said, speaking almost without moving her lips. She nodded slightly in the direction of the parking lot.

Ed looked over.

"Don't look!" the woman hissed.

"Now, Martha, would you please tell me how I'm supposed to see them if I don't look?" Ed asked.

"Just glance over there," Martha insisted. "You don't have to be obvious about it."

Ed followed her instructions and saw the two men.

"All right, I see them," he said. "Now what?"

"Don't you find them frightening?"

"Not particularly."

4

Martha shivered. "Well, I do. And I'm glad we aren't out here after dark."

"Don't be silly. We're in one of the nicest areas in the city."

"It wouldn't matter if we were in St. Patrick's Cathedral, those two are frightening."

"Because they're black? That's pretty prejudicial, isn't it?"

"Black has nothing to do with it. I'm telling you, those two are up to no good." When Ed looked toward them again, Martha hissed, "Don't look! If they see us looking at them, they could get angry. There's no telling what they might do." •

"Hell, I'm not the one looking at them, Martha, you are." Ed chuckled. "I wouldn't be surprised if they didn't think you were trying to pick them up."

"Ed, don't say such a thing!" Martha gasped, pointedly looking away.

At that moment Bart Eberwine and George Kinder, members of the Executive Stress Athletic Club, came through the side door of the club, which opened onto the parking lot. Both men were athletically trim and had healthy tans. There was a yuppielike sameness in their appearance, differentiated only because Eberwine was blond and Kinder had dark hair.

They were carrying small athletic bags and

racquets. Kinder raised his racquet over his head and took several quick steps to one side, then made a demonstration swing.

"I don't know," he said. "My timing was off. I didn't begin to warm up until the end. I could've taken you best three out of five."

"No way," Eberwine replied, laughing. "I would've creamed you no matter how many games we played." He noticed the two black men moving from the Dumpster toward Kinder's silver BMW. "Hey, George," he said, putting a hand on his companion's arm, the two stopping in the lot. "Who are those guys by your Beamer?"

Kinder looked up. "I don't know. Probably a couple of guys wanting to make a little money cleaning it up. They come around all the time."

"Yeah? Well, they've got no business being in here," Eberwine said. "We pay plenty to belong to this club. The least they can do is keep the riffraff out of the parking lot."

"Don't be so uptight about it," Kinder said easily. "They aren't causing any problem."

"They've got no business being there," Eberwine repeated. "Hey!" he called to the two men as he walked in their direction. "Get your black asses away from that car!"

"Say what?" one of the men replied.

"You heard me, nigger," Eberwine said. "I said get your black ass away from that car."

6

"Bart, will you calm down for chrissake," Kinder said nervously, a few steps behind. "What are you trying to do?"

Eberwine waved Kinder's protestations aside. "Let me handle this. What are you looking for, the welfare office?" he shouted to the men. "It's nowhere around here."

"Say, you got a problem, white boy?" one of the black men asked, starting toward Eberwine, who'd stopped ten feet from the car, along with Kinder.

"I don't have a problem. You do," Eberwine said, putting down his bag and pointing to the man. "I'm going to whip your nigger ass if you don't get the hell out of here."

"You want some of this nigger ass, motherfucker," standing a few feet away now, "you come get it!"

"Oh Jesus! What's going on here?" Kinder muttered, afraid. "Bart, will you shut the fuck up! You guys, listen, don't pay any attention to him." He pulled two twenty dollar bills from his billfold, then stepped up to the more belligerent of the two black men. "Here, take this money for your troubles."

"Get away from me, motherfucker!"

Following her own admonition against looking, Martha had seen nothing of the confrontation that broke out between the two white men

7

and the two black men. They had nearly passed the lot, and she'd almost managed to put them out of her mind, when she heard two short, flat, loud pops.

"Ed!" she gasped, turning. "What was that?"

"Gunshots," Ed answered. He, too, turned to see what was happening.

They saw two men down, one white and one black. The other black man was running straight for them.

"Oh, my God, Ed, he's coming after us!" Martha shouted, taking a step back on the sidewalk.

Ed wasn't worried about the fleeing black man. He was more concerned with the fact that the white man had a gun raised as if about to shoot, and if he did, he and Martha would be in the line of fire.

"Martha, get down!" He grabbed his wife reflexively and pulled her down to the sidewalk with him. Fortunately, the white man lowered his gun without firing again.

When Phil Cerreta's unmarked, black four-door Ford came to a stop, he and his partner, Mike Logan, got out to survey the scene.

"Jesus," Logan said. "Two dead. What? Are they coming in pairs now?"

"It's called economy of effort," Cerreta replied sarcastically. "We can work two for the price of one."

A uniformed cop who was already on the scene came over to the car and hit the hood with his nightstick.

"You can't park here, this part of the lot is closed," the cop said.

Cerreta was in his forties, stocky, with broad shoulders, a full chest, and a slight belly rise. He had dark, curly hair and a round face. Logan, Cerreta's younger partner, was also dark-haired, but was somewhat taller, slimmer, and with a longer face. They were both expressive men, and if necessary, both could show incredible hardness. The most notable thing about their faces, however, was the similarity—not in their features, but in their demeanor. There was something about them that said they had seen it all. It was the universal expression of a homicide detective, and the uniform cop recognized it at once, even though he didn't know them personally. He backed away from his challenging posture.

"Sorry," he said. "I didn't know you guys were suits."

"I'm Sergeant Cerreta, this is Detective Logan. We're from Homicide." Cerreta showed his badge, then took a quick glance around. "What've we got here, officer?"

"Two bodies, one a vic, one a perp," the

uniform answered laconically. "The vic was stabbed, the perp was shot. But I don't know why they sent you guys down here. We ain't got nothing here for you."

"What, are we missing something here?" Logan asked. "You just said two are dead. We're Homicide. Who should be here? Traffic?"

"Traffic's already here," the uniform replied. "What I mean is, it's an open and shut case. One of the bad guys stabs one of the good guys. Then, 'bang,' the other good guy takes out the bad guy. You ask me, the shooter's a hero. The mayor ought to pin a medal on him."

"It's a little early to be handing out medals, don't you think?" Logan asked.

"Not in my book," the uniform insisted. "Not in hers either." He pointed to a television reporter who was already interviewing the shooter.

"Shit," Logan said, turning his back to the reporter to face Cerreta. "You know who that is, don't you? That's Joanna Blaylock. She's been on a police- and city-hall-bashing bandwagon for the last six months."

"Yeah, I've seen some of her stuff," Cerreta said. "You want to know the kicker? My wife thinks she's great, a role model for young girls."

"She's hell on wheels," Logan said. "You see

the way she grilled that congressman over the check-bouncing thing? She put his balls in a vise and squeezed."

Cerreta chuckled. "He had over a thousand bad checks. His balls shoulda been in a vise. You or I did that, we'd be kicked off the force."

"Yeah, well, what I'm saying is, watch your ass around her," Logan warned.

Cerreta looked over at the man Joanna Blaylock was interviewing. "What's the shooter's name?" he asked the uniformed cop.

The officer checked his notebook. "His name is Eberwine, Bart Eberwine. The vic is George Kinder. Eberwine and Kinder were both brokers in the investing firm of . . ." He looked at his notebook again. "Barry, Patmore and Daigh, that's D-A-I-G-H. That's on Sixth Avenue."

"Did you say there were *two* perps?" Cerreta asked.

"Yeah."

"What happened to the other one?"

"He was real brave. He started running when the shooting started."

"Any witnesses?" Logan asked. He pointed toward Eberwine, who at that moment was speaking into the television interviewer's microphone. "I mean besides Wyatt Earp over there."

"Sort of," the uniform replied. "A couple of

tourists saw the two black guys hanging around in the parking lot before anything happened. They didn't see the actual incident, but they heard the shooting and looked around in time to see the perp that got away." He referred again to his notebook. "Their names are Ed and Martha Bowers and they're from Muncie, Indiana. They're both retired school teachers."

"You want the tourists or Eberwine first?" Cerreta asked Logan.

"I'll take the tourists," Logan said.

The detectives got out of the car. Cerreta went over to interview Eberwine, but the television interview was still in progress.

Joanna Blaylock was an exceptionally attractive woman. She was a Cheryl Tiegs lookalike who may have gotten her job as a result of her looks, but was determined to prove to the world —or at least to the New York viewers—that she deserved it. Her investigative reporting style was very aggressive and had already won her one Emmy, while building a large and loyal group of fans. It had also improved the ratings of the TV station where she worked.

By coincidence, this very morning, Cerreta had seen a huge billboard promotion of her on the side of a building over on Third Avenue. It featured a dramatic action photo, Blaylock holding a microphone in the foreground while a fire engine and several firemen fought a blaz-

ing inferno behind her. Cerreta could even recognize the scene. The burning building was the
First Seaboard Savings and Trust Company, and
it had been located on Third Avenue, just half a
block from where the billboard sensationalizing
it was now placed.

WHEN IT HAPPENS IN NEW YORK, JOANNA BLAYLOCK AND
WACN DYNAMIC NEWS WILL BRING IT HOME TO YOU! the
billboard proclaimed in bold letters.

"Were you frightened, Mr. Eberwine?" Cerreta heard Blaylock ask as he arrived. She held
the microphone up in front of Eberwine's face.

"Yes, of course I was frightened. Who
wouldn't be under such circumstances? But
controlled fright can give one certain advantages—heightened awareness, heightened
senses, that sort of thing. I thought of that and
used the fright to my accretion."

Accretion? Cerreta thought. He winced.
What sort of pompous confidence would allow
a man to use a word like that?

"Even so, seeing two men coming for you
with knives would immobilize most people,
would it not?" Blaylock asked.

"Many people, yes . . . and perhaps even
most. But not all. For example, think of all
those soldiers who have performed bravely in
combat, think of the policemen who face this
sort of thing every day, or the firemen who

must run into burning buildings. And of course, airline pilots and cabin attendants have also performed bravely under conditions of extreme fear," Eberwine went on. "One can develop a certain discipline of mental and emotional toughness which can be called upon in such situations. In my own case, I have learned that if one is to survive in any endeavor —be it business or coping with the stress of life in the city—mental toughness is the best asset one can have. It would be nice if we had someone to turn to in such circumstances, but more often than not we must face these stressful situations alone. When that happens, it's necessary to take matters into your own hands, and mental toughness will allow you to do that."

"How is it, Mr. Eberwine, that you were carrying a gun? Guns are illegal, are they not?" she asked.

"Well, yes, they are illegal for the average citizen. But I'm licensed to carry a gun," Eberwine explained. "You see, in my job I'm sometimes required to carry large sums of money. By coincidence, today was such a day."

"A fortunate coincidence for you," Blaylock said. "Unfortunate for the street toughs who attacked you."

"Unfortunate, yes, I would say that best describes this whole tragic experience. What happened here today was the stuff of nightmares. It was certainly not the kind of thing one would want to go through.''

Cerreta, watching and listening to the interview, frowned, and began to scratch the side of his nose. During his years on the force, he had known many officers who were involved in shootings. Different officers reacted to it differently. Some were so pumped up from an adrenaline high that it was almost impossible to talk to them. Others experienced a period of shock, regret, even remorse. Recognizing such reactions was a part of his job, and Cerreta had become good at dealing with it.

Eberwine was pumped up—not as much as some, but certainly enough to be noticeable, which seemed normal to the detective. The man exhibited a little fear, but it was under control. He showed some remorse . . . though that, too, he held well in check. He was cool and composed, presenting the right appearance; not a hair was mussed or an item of his expensive, but casual, clothing wrinkled. Eberwine's voice was perfectly modulated between determination and regret, as if he had been thrust by circumstances into this position but had the confidence to handle it. In fact, Eberwine fit the profile to a T. His physical and emotional reaction to what happened was exactly what all the books and articles said would be normal for the average person under similar circumstances. There was not one anomaly or aberration. There was nothing, absolutely nothing, out of place.

So why, Cerreta wondered, was his nose itching?

Joanna Blaylock turned to face the camera.

"New Yorkers have grown accustomed to the idea that there are certain areas of the city that have been taken over by the lawless elements. Even the police admit that they cannot control crime in these high-profile danger areas. But this . . ." She turned to look over her shoulder toward the parking lot. "This is the parking lot of a very exclusive athletic club, hardly the typical location for a mugging. Because Mr. Eberwine was armed, he managed to fight off the muggers, killing one and driving the other away. But what of those citizens who face the same nightmare and are not armed? If the police are unable to protect them, what recourse have they?

"Tragically, even though Mr. Eberwine was armed, he was unable to prevent the killing of his friend, the man with whom he had just played racquetball. As a result, his friend, whose identity we cannot divulge until his next of kin has been notified, has become one more cipher in the toll of killings in the street. He is number 257 so far this year. But that doesn't tell the whole story about the man. To his family, to

Bart Eberwine—who risked his own life fighting for his friend—he is a human being . . . a human being who met a tragic and very untimely end.''

She waited for a long beat, staring intently at the camera before she affixed her closing tag.

"This is Joanna Blaylock, WACN Dynamic News. . . . Did you get that, Billy?" she asked, when the cameraman lowered his camera.

"Got it, Joanna," the cameraman answered. "It'll be a great piece."

"Thanks." She saw Cerreta waiting on the side, flashed him a big smile and brushed a fall of strawberry-blond hair back from the side of her face. "He's all yours," she said brightly.

"Thank you," Cerreta replied. "By the way, Miss Blaylock, as a matter of curiosity, would you mind telling me how you got here so fast?"

"It's called professionalism," she said. "You ought to try it sometime. Who are you with, anyway? One of the newspapers?"

"No," Cerreta answered, without being specific.

When Blaylock looked at him more closely, she saw the badge folder hanging from his jacket pocket. "Wait a minute," she said. She pointed a polished fingernail at him. "I've met you before. You're Lieutenant Cerecca?"

"Sergeant Cerreta."

"Cerreta, yes. We ran into each other at the

17

elevator murder last month. Have you found the person who did it?"

"It's still under investigation," Cerreta admitted.

"But of course it is," she said patronizingly. "There are several that are 'still under investigation,' I believe. At least that's the standard answer I get when I check on the status of these uncleared cases." She looked over toward the two bodies. "You shouldn't have any trouble with this one. The victim and the perpetrator are both dead. Wouldn't it be nice if all of your cases were tied up in neat little packages like this?"

Cerreta's jaw hardened. "I don't call two dead a 'neat little package,' " he replied. "Now, if you'll excuse me, Miss Blaylock, I do have work to do." He turned to Eberwine. "Mr. Eberwine, I'd like to ask you a few questions."

During the entire exchange between Cerreta and Joanna Blaylock, Bart Eberwine had been leaning against the side of the silver BMW with his arms folded across his chest. He was watching, almost dispassionately, as other policemen took pictures, made measurements, and examined the two bodies which were still sprawled on the ground, exactly as they had fallen.

"How much longer are the bodies going to have to stay out here like this?" Eberwine asked Cerreta.

Cerreta looked over at the activity. "Not too much longer," he answered. "Mr. Eberwine, I'd like you to tell me what happened."

Eberwine sighed. "I told the uniformed policeman what happened, and I told the TV reporter. Couldn't you just get the information from one of the ones I've already spoken to?"

"I'm afraid not. You'll have to tell me."

"All right," Eberwine said. "George and I had just finished playing racquetball. We play . . ." He paused and pressed his knuckles into his forehead again, then amended his statement. "That is, we *played* every Wednesday afternoon."

"You must be pretty good at it if you play every Wednesday," Cerreta said.

"I am." Eberwine nodded toward George Kinder's body. "So was George. We had very competitive, you might even say, very heated, games."

"Heated?"

"Like I said, the games were very competitive."

"Did you ever fight over them?"

"Depends on what you mean by fight," Eberwine replied. "Sometimes we would have some pretty spirited discussions."

"What about today's game? Did you have a spirited discussion?"

"No, not really." Eberwine looked at Cerreta. "What are you implying, Sergeant?"

"I wasn't implying anything, Mr. Eberwine," Cerreta said. "I'm just trying to get a feel for what happened, that's all. So, after the game, you came out to the parking lot."

"Yes."

"Then what happened?"

"We saw two men approaching George's car. This man lying here, and the one who ran."

"You said they were approaching the car. Approaching from where?"

"I'm not sure. I think they had been standing over there by the Dumpster."

"As they approached the car, were they making any threatening moves, toward you or toward the car?"

"Well, no, not at first," Eberwine admitted. "Not until I yelled at them."

"You yelled at them?"

"You're damned right I did," Eberwine replied.

"What, exactly, did you yell?"

"I told them to get their black asses away from the car."

"What happened next?"

"They got very belligerent," Eberwine said. "They started calling us names."

"Like what?"

"It's a pretty graphic name."

"I'm a big boy, I've heard graphic language before."

"They called us motherfuckers."

"All right, you called them names, they called you names. How did it get from name-calling to this?" He pointed to the two bodies.

"One of them, that one," Eberwine said, "came toward us with a knife. George jumped between us to try and stop him."

"How was he planning to do that?"

"With money," Eberwine said. He shook his head. "Poor George, he thought he could buy his way into or out of anything. Anyway, he was holding two twenty-dollar bills out toward the two black guys, trying to talk them into going away, but they wouldn't have any of it. The next thing I know, George is down on the ground. When I saw the guy coming toward me, I shot him."

"You shot him?"

"Yes."

"Where was the gun all this time?"

"I beg your pardon?"

"When you first challenged the two black guys, did you have the gun in your hand? Did they know you were armed?"

"No," Eberwine said.

"Why not? Wouldn't that have made your point?"

"I didn't think I would need it," Eberwine

21

replied. "Besides, I don't carry the gun as a means of issuing threats. The gun is supposed to be for self-defense."

"So, where was the gun while all the posturing was going on?"

"It was in my athletic bag," Eberwine said.

"Do you take the gun with you every time you play racquetball?"

"No," Eberwine replied. "But this afternoon it just so happened that I made a large money transfer, so I had to have the gun with me. I was taking the gun home, and I thought it would be better to keep it in the athletic bag than to leave it in the car. Like Miss Blaylock said, it was just one of those fortunate coincidences."

"Fortunate coincidences . . ." Cerreta said. "Tell me, Mr. Eberwine, if you had not been carrying the gun today, do you think this would have happened?"

"What do you mean?"

"Isn't it just possible that the thought of having that gun handy made you just a little more combative? If you had not been armed and the two men had been standing there—"

"Would I have just let it go, you mean, and said nothing?" Eberwine asked.

"Yes."

Eberwine thought for a long moment. "I honestly don't know the answer to that question. Perhaps, subconsciously, knowing that I had the gun made me a little more sure of myself," he admitted. "Whatever it was that gave me the courage, I don't knock it. I mean, someone has to stand up to these hoodlums somewhere, don't you think? Otherwise, they're going to take the streets away from the decent people."

"But standing up to them didn't stop them, did it?" Cerreta asked.

"No," Eberwine said. "It didn't stop them."

"And it got your friend killed."

"Are you blaming me for that?" Eberwine asked.

"I'm just suggesting that there might have been a better way to handle this."

"Sergeant . . . you did say Sergeant, didn't you?" Eberwine started, making the word sound almost servile. "I am not ashamed of my performance here this afternoon. In fact, I believe that under the circumstances, I handled myself quite admirably. So, if you're trying to make me feel guilty about showing a little intestinal fortitude, you aren't going to."

"Trying to make you feel guilty isn't my job, Mr. Eberwine," Cerreta said easily. "Now, how about the man who ran? Can you describe him?"

"Not very well, I'm afraid," Eberwine said.

Cerreta was surprised. "Well, surely you noticed something about him?"

23

"He was a black male."

"Black male. That doesn't give us much to go on, does it?" Cerreta said. "Was he bigger or smaller than this man?"

"Bigger, I think. No, maybe smaller."

"Any scars, or distinguishing features?"

"I don't know," Eberwine said. "I wish I could help you, but he wasn't around for long. He ran."

"I see. Now, for the record, Mr. Eberwine, which one of the two men stabbed Kinder?"

"This one," Eberwine said, pointing to the body.

"Did the other one also have a knife?"

"I . . . I think so. However, I wouldn't swear to it. Like I said, as soon as everything started, he ran."

"When did he run? When he saw your gun or when you began shooting?"

"I'm not sure."

"Did you shoot at the one who ran?"

"No. I started to, I aimed at him, but there were some people in my line of fire." He looked over toward the two tourists who at that moment were talking to Logan. "Those people," he said, pointing at them. "I didn't want to take a chance on hitting them, so I lowered my gun."

"All right, that'll be all for now," Cerreta said. "Thank you for your time."

As Cerreta turned to leave Eberwine, Joanna Blaylock came up to him.

"Detective, wait a minute, I want to apologize for my behavior before," she said. "I know you have a difficult job to do and pushy broads don't make it easier. Do you forgive me?" She flashed her most appealing smile.

"Don't worry about it," Cerreta said. "When you've been bombarded with brickbats, a few little Ping-Pong balls don't bother you at all."

"I suppose in your line of work you've had to take some abuse," she replied. "Physical as well as verbal. Listen, could I ask you a few questions?"

"I'd rather not, right now," Cerreta replied.

"But don't you think the people have a right to know about this full-scale war we're having in our streets?" she insisted. "And I would think that as bad as something like this makes the police look—that our citizens have to arm themselves for their own protection—the police would want their side of the story heard."

Cerreta had started to walk away, but he stopped and looked back at her. "We don't *have* a side of the story, Miss Blaylock," he growled. "It isn't us *against* the people, it's us *with* the people. Now if you would excuse me, perhaps we can gain a little ground on this 'war in the streets' you media people keep harping about."

"You think it's something we made up?" she

asked. "Don't you believe there *is* a war going on in our streets today? Muggings, rape, violent crimes of all sort, including murder, are steadily on the rise. If this isn't war in the streets, what would you call it?"

"We're no different from any other city. We do have a problem," Cerreta admitted, "though I'd have to think about it before I'd say it has reached the proportions of a revolution. But we're doing the best we can, Miss Blaylock, so if you would excuse me, I do have some work to do."

"Thank you, Sergeant Cerreta," she said. There was a triumphant smile on her face, which Cerreta found puzzling until, out of the corner of his eye, he saw the cameraman lowering his camera. Everything he'd just said had been captured on tape.

"I did not grant an interview, Miss Blaylock," he said.

"You didn't have to, Sergeant," she shot back. "That wasn't an interview. It was more on the order of what we call an 'actuality,' a 'sound bite' of one of our public servants at work. You are a public servant, aren't you?"

Cerreta was about to argue, then shrugged his shoulders. What the hell? He knew he hadn't said anything that he shouldn't have said. Let her have the tape, he thought. She wouldn't be able to get any mileage out of it.

Leaving Joanna Blaylock and her cameraman behind, Cerreta walked over to the police van. The back door was open and there were four plastic bags sitting on the van floor. One of the bags contained a 9mm Berreta; the second, two spent nine-millimeter shell casings; a third, a billfold, keys, and a handful of coins taken from George Kinder's body. The final bag contained items taken from the body of the black man; coins, a comb, and some money, kept in a roll by a thick rubber band.

"No billfold on this guy?" Cerreta asked the policeman who was detailed to keep an eye on the physical evidence as it was gathered.

"Nope. Just what you see there."

Cerreta counted $480 in twenty-dollar bills.

"Nice piece of pocket change," he said.

"Yeah, tell me about it," the cop replied.

Cerreta looked around the back of the van. "Where's the knife?" he asked.

"What knife?"

"The knife that was used in the stabbing."

The policeman looked at his clipboard. "I don't know, Sergeant. There's no knife on the inventory list, so that means no one has brought one to me."

"There has to be a knife."

Cerreta walked back over to the police hearse just as they were about to load the bodies. The photographer and one of the crime-lab men were standing there.

"I didn't see the knife over with the physical evidence," he said. "Any of you come up with it?"

"Not yet," one of them admitted. "Though we have been looking for it."

"Look around again," Cerreta ordered. "It has to be here somewhere." Then Cerreta joined Logan, who was questioning the two tourists.

"This is Ed and Martha Bowers," his partner said. "Neither one of them saw what actually happened, but they're both able to give pretty good descriptions of the guy who ran."

"Where were you?" Cerreta asked the couple.

"Over there," Martha replied, pointing to the farthermost corner of the parking lot.

"That's pretty far away to be able to tell too much about how a person looks, isn't it?"

"He ran right past us, officer," Ed explained. "As close to us as you are now."

"Besides, we walked by them a bit earlier," Martha explained. "I knew then that they were up to no good."

"How did you know that, Mrs. Bowers?"

"I beg your pardon?"

"How did you know they were up to no good?

28

Were they behaving in some way that tipped you off?''

"Well, no, not exactly," she hedged. "But you could tell that they didn't belong there. And I don't even mean the way they looked, or the way they were dressed. I'm talking about the way they were acting.''

"How were they acting?''

"I don't know. Sort of nervous, like they were waiting for something. And they kept looking around, like they knew they didn't belong there.''

"I see. Well, let's get to the description, shall we?''

"You mean the one who ran?''

Cerreta smiled. "Yes, ma'am," he answered. "We know what the other one looks like. We have him over there.''

"Yes, of course," Martha said sheepishly. "Well, I'll start with how he was dressed. He was wearing khaki pants, tennis shoes, and a tee shirt.''

"Hoya," Ed interjected.

"I beg your pardon?''

"The tee shirt was a Hoya shirt," Ed said. "You know, the Georgetown Hoyas? It was white, printed in blue. It has a drawing of a bulldog, wearing one of those hats that the underclassmen used to wear.''

"A beanie," Martha added.

"Yes, a beanie," Ed said. "The bulldog is wearing a beanie with the word Georgetown printed on it."

"Did you notice anything else about him? His size, for example?"

"Of course I did," Ed said. "He was five-nine, fairly muscular, between 170 and 175 pounds."

Cerreta looked up in surprise. "That's pretty specific, Mr. Bowers."

"I thought you wanted me to be specific."

"Yes, but how can you be so positive?"

"Sizing up people used to be my job," Ed said.

"I beg your pardon?"

"Mr. Bowers was a high school basketball coach," Logan explained.

"Two state championships," Bowers added proudly. "So I'm pretty good at gauging a person's size. This guy was a guard."

"And don't forget his eyes," Martha added. "I've never seen such eyes."

"What about the man's eyes?"

"It was the color," Martha said. "I guess, technically, they were brown. I mean, black people do have brown eyes, don't they? But I've never seen such a distinctive shade of brown. It was more of a yellow than a brown."

"Yellowish-brown," Cerreta said.

"Yes," Martha replied. "Oh, I know something I didn't think of when I was talking to you,

Officer Logan," she added. "I think I can show you the exact color, if you would like to see it."

"Yes, sure, we'd like to see it," Logan said.

Martha reached into the sack she was carrying and took out a small box. It held a brooch encrusted with five gemstones.

"This is what they call a mother's brooch," Martha explained. "You see, it has my birthstone, Ed's birthstone, and a birthstone for each of our three children."

"Yes, ma'am."

"Jennifer," Martha said.

"I beg your pardon?"

"Our oldest daughter, Jennifer, was born in November," Martha said, pointing to her daughter's stone. "Topaz. That was the color of the man's eyes."

"You drive," Cerreta said.

"All right," Logan replied, sliding behind the wheel. "Sure would be nice if they were all this easy, wouldn't it? One dead perp and a good description of the one who ran."

"Yeah," Cerreta said. "I guess so."

"You guess so? What do you mean, you guess so? Something bothering you?"

"No, not really." Cerreta stroked his chin. "But I would like to know where the hell the knife is."

"Yeah, well, it'll probably turn up."

31

"Probably," Cerreta agreed. He turned and looked back toward the parking lot. Eberwine was about to step into a taxicab, and he brushed his hair back as he did. Cerreta scratched his nose. "He's a cool son of a bitch, isn't he?"

"Who, Eberwine?" Logan asked.

"Yes." Cerreta turned back around.

"I suppose he is," Logan answered. "But don't forget, he's one of those Wall Street geniuses who can drop three million bucks in one afternoon without batting an eye. That takes a special breed."

"Genius, huh? How do you know he's a genius?"

"I talked to some of the other club members," Logan said. "Without exception they were ready to tell me what a brilliant businessman this guy is."

"Uh-huh," Cerreta grunted. He scratched his nose again.

"Eberwine is the true American hero," Logan went on. "He is not only the embodiment of the productive capitalist, he has defended himself, and all productive Americans, by force of arms, against a representative of that great, unwashed class of have-nots who think society owes them a living. Hell, the way things are going, folks will be running Eberwine for president pretty soon."

Cerreta laughed. "What a crock of shit."

"Maybe so," Logan agreed, also laughing. He looked over toward his partner. "But seriously, Phil, I don't get the feeling that anything is particularly wrong here. Do you?"

"I wouldn't exactly call it a feeling," Cerreta said. "It's more of an itch."

Chapter Two

Captain Cragen brushed his hand over the top of his head, possibly a residual habit from the days when he actually had hair. Cerreta was standing near the file cabinet in the captain's office, and Logan was leaning against the door with his arms folded across his chest.

"Did you see the *Post* this morning?" Cragen asked, tossing the tabloid onto his desk.

"I'm not sure I want to," Cerreta replied, but he picked it up anyway. "Christ, will you look at that headline? 'Citizen Hero Kills Mugger.' "

Logan chuckled. "I told you. If he keeps this up, he'll be running for office."

"Everybody loves a hero," Cerreta suggested.

"Any make on our John Doe yet?" Logan asked.

"Not yet," Cragen answered. "But we're running a match on the fingerprints. If he has any record at all—and I'd be willing to bet that he does—we'll make him."

"I'd sure like to have a name for him," Logan said.

"Yes, and while we're making up the wish list, I'd like to have the knife," Cerreta added.

"You sure you guys looked everywhere?" Cragen asked. "Maybe it's under one of the cars, behind a wheel or something."

"No, we looked," Cerreta said. "I got down and crawled around. It wasn't anywhere around there."

"There were several citizens there when we arrived. Maybe one of them picked it up," Logan suggested.

"Why the hell would anyone do that?" Cerreta asked.

"Who knows? There are some weird people in the world. One of them may have wanted a souvenir."

There was a knock on the door, and when Logan opened it, the desk sergeant leaned his head in.

"Pardon me, Captain, but I was just wondering if any of you guys caught Phil's interview on the evening news last night?"

"My interview?" Cerreta replied. "What interview?"

The desk sergeant chuckled. "I don't know," he answered. "How many did you give?" He held up a video cassette. "I taped the newscast last night and brought it in this morning just in case someone didn't see it."

"Damned big of you, Tim," Cerreta growled.

"Did you grant an interview?" Cragen asked.

"Not willingly," Cerreta answered. "Though that newswoman, Joanna Blaylock, did start talking to me, and when we were finished, I saw that her cameraman had his camera going. But there can't be too much to it."

"There's more than you think," Tim said. "I think you'd better take a look at it. I've got it cued up to the piece."

"Do you mind, Captain?" Cerreta asked, pointing to the combination TV and VCR unit in Cragen's office.

"By all means," the captain replied. "I'd like to see it myself."

The picture that came up was of a silver-gray-haired studio anchorman with perfect teeth and a practiced expression. His tone was deep, professional, and concerned.

"Death continues to stalk the streets of New York," he began solemnly. "Today it came to midtown Manhattan. Joanna Blaylock was on the scene, and she files this report."

The picture on the screen switched to the parking lot of the Executive Stress Athletic Club. In the background two bodies were titillatingly visible, though not so obvious as to be distasteful. In the foreground was Joanna Blaylock. She was holding a microphone in front of her face, staring at the camera. Her strawberry hair was just slightly windblown, and her green eyes were sparkling with intensity. She looked like a woman who was trying to appear more professional than beautiful, but somehow managed to do both.

"Today all New Yorkers may take heart that there was a small victory for the common man," she began. "Bart Eberwine is an ordinary citizen, a broker for the firm of Barry, Patmore and Daigh. An ordinary citizen, yes, but what happened to him today was anything but ordinary. It all began as he was leaving the Executive Stress Athletic Club with a friend and coworker.

"They were approached by two as yet unidentified muggers.

"Who knows what the muggers had in mind? They certainly did not count upon the bravery of Mr. Eberwine . . . nor did they realize that because of a position which often requires him to handle large sums of money, Mr. Eberwine is licensed to carry firearms. As a result, one of the muggers was killed and the other driven away. The tragic side of the story, however, is that Mr. Eberwine's friend and coworker was stabbed and killed by the same man who was himself shot and killed by Mr. Eberwine.''

The scene then switched to her interview with Eberwine.

"Were you frightened, Mr. Eberwine?" She held the microphone in front of his face.

"Controlled fright can give one certain advantages—heightened awareness, heightened senses, that sort of thing. I thought of that and used the fright to my accretion.''

"Even so, seeing two men coming for you with knives drawn would immobilize most people, wouldn't it?"

"One can develop a certain discipline of mental and emotional toughness which can be called upon in such situations. In my own case, I have learned that if one is to survive in any endeavor—be it business or coping with the stress of life in the city—mental toughness is the best asset one can have. It would be nice if we had someone to turn to in such circumstances, but more often than not we must face these stressful situations alone. When that happens, it's necessary to take matters into your own hands, and mental toughness will allow you to do that.''

"Unfortunate for the street toughs who attacked you,'' Blaylock said.

"Yes," Eberwine replied.

"Damn," Cerreta said. "You know, Captain, I watched that entire interview being taped and I don't remember it coming out quite like that."

Joanna Blaylock turned to face the camera.

"New Yorkers have grown accustomed to the idea that there are certain areas of the city that have been taken over by the lawless elements. Even the police admit that they cannot control crime in these high-profile danger areas. But this . . ." she turned to look over her shoulder toward the parking lot. "This is the parking lot of a very exclusive athletic club, hardly the typical location for a mugging. Because Mr. Eberwine was armed, he managed to fight off the muggers, killing one and driving the other away. But what of those citizens who face the same nightmare and are not armed? With the police unable to protect us, what recourse have we?

"I spoke today with Detective Sergeant Phil Cerreta, one of the police officers working the case. I must explain to our viewers that Sergeant Cerreta did not know the camera was running. That will, no doubt, explain his unusually candid response."

"What unusually candid response?" Cerreta asked. "I didn't make any unusually candid response. What is she talking about?"

"I have a feeling we are about to find out," Cragen suggested.

Blaylock's image was replaced by Cerreta's. Beneath his picture was the caption: *Detective Sergeant Phil Cerreta, Homicide, NYPD.*

"We do have a problem," Cerreta said. "I'd say it has reached the proportions of a revolution. But we're doing the best we can."

"What?" Cerreta exploded. He pointed to the TV monitor. "Captain Cragen, I didn't say that!"

The shot of Cerreta was replaced by a close-up of Joanna Blaylock.

"How bad has the problem become?" she asked the viewers. "As you just heard, even the police admit that we are facing a revolution, a revolution that has spilled beyond the ghetto and into our most affluent areas. As a result, the toll of killings in the streets of this city continues to mount, and the police, apparently, are unable to do anything to stop it. Is it any wonder then that ordinary citizens like Mr. Eberwine feel constrained to arm themselves for their own protection?"

She waited for a long beat, staring intently at the camera before she affixed her closing tag.

"This is Joanna Blaylock, WACN Dynamic News."

The picture returned to the silver-haired anchorman in the studio.

"In other news, Bernard Shipley, former CEO of Sterns and Lowe, charged that Angelo Costaconti, reputed Mafia boss, is laundering ill-gotten money through various Wall Street investment firms. However, Security Exchange Commission spokesman James Russell denied Shipley's charge, stating that—" Cragen turned the TV off in mid-sentence.

"Captain, I—I swear I didn't say that," Cerreta sputtered, pointing to the screen. "I don't know where the hell she got that."

"Oh? You mean that wasn't you?" Cragen asked.

"Well, yes, it was me, but I didn't say that. I don't know how she did it, but somehow my words have been changed."

Cragen sighed, then punched the tape out of the VCR. "I know you didn't say that, Phil," the captain replied. "You are the victim of 'creative' editing."

"I hope the people downtown realize that," Cerreta said.

"I'll speak with the chief," Cragen promised. "He can't be thrilled about this sort of thing, but I'll assure him the tape was doctored."

"Do you think he'll believe you?"

"He'll believe me. He knows you, *and* he knows Joanna Blaylock."

"Isn't there anything we can do about that woman?" Logan asked.

Cragen looked at him. "Like what?"

"Maybe we could shoot her," Logan teased.

Cragen laughed. "If you did, I could almost guarantee you that the review board would call it a good shoot."

"Maybe we could persuade the TV station to play the unedited version or something," Logan suggested. "You know, appeal to their sense of fair play to show both sides?"

"That would be asking a lot," Cerreta said. "If they played the unedited tape, it would completely discredit the report she just aired."

Captain Cragen nodded. "Which is exactly why the station won't do it. Joanna Blaylock is an Emmy winner and a numbers getter. The station is going to protect her."

"Can't we force the issue?" Logan asked.

"Force the issue? How?"

"Subpoena the tape," Logan suggested.

Cragen shook his head. "We've tried, unsuccessfully, to get unedited tape in the past."

"Why haven't we been successful?" Logan asked. "The principle of the confidentiality of a news source has never been established."

"Hell, most of the time they don't even try that tactic anymore," Cragen said. "They just tape over the raw footage so that it no longer exists."

"Is that legal?"

"They claim they do it as an economy measure. Once they get the edited version, they can reuse the tape the raw version was on."

"That's bullshit."

"It may be," Cragen said. "But it is effective bullshit."

"Yeah, well, I can't be worrying about something I have no control over," Cerreta said. "I think I'll see what I can find out about Eberwine."

"Eberwine?" The captain was surprised. "Why do you want to waste time on him? If you want to get this case wrapped up, and off the front pages, find the perp who ran."

"Don't worry, don't worry, we will," Cerreta promised. "But I don't want to just walk away from Eberwine."

"Phil, am I missing something here?" Cragen asked. "Are there a couple of pieces of this puzzle that aren't coming together?"

"I don't know."

"You don't know? What do you mean, you don't know?"

Logan chuckled. "He has an itch."

Cragen looked at his two officers, then ran his hand over the top of his bald head and let out a long sigh.

"All right," he finally said. "I've known you long enough to know that when you get a notion like this, more often than not there's something behind it. Though I wish you would tell me what it is.''

"I wish I could, Captain," Cerreta replied. "But it's like I told Mike, I don't understand myself what there is about this case . . . It's like I have an itch, but I don't know where to scratch."

"Come on, admit it, you just don't like Eberwine," Logan suggested.

"No, I don't," Cerreta replied. "I think he's an arrogant, self-centered, oil-smooth son of a bitch. And I admit I don't like him. But I don't think that's what's causing me to want to take a closer look before we close the books on this."

Cragen rubbed his chin and sighed. "All right, Phil, have a closer look. The books will stay open until you two bring in the other mugger. But don't drag your feet on this—you heard Joanna Blaylock. She's using a simple parking-lot mugging to spread her revolution bullshit. Find the other man, bring him in, and let's get this case closed."

"Think I'll get some coffee," Logan said when the two men returned to their desks. "Want me to bring you a cup?"

"Yeah, thanks."

Minutes later, when Logan reached Cerreta's desk with two cups of coffee, Cerreta was on the phone. He covered the mouthpiece with his hand.

"Thanks."

"Who you talkin' to?"

"Sarah Potts, down in records," Cerreta said. He took a swallow then spoke into the phone. "Yes, E-B-E-R-W-I-N-E. Bart, or maybe Bartholomew. What do you have on him? He has a permit to carry a pistol, so there must have been some investigation made."

"Yes, here it is," Sarah replied. "One non-moving traffic violation, one complaint from a neighbor for playing his stereo too loud, and . . . this is odd."

"What is?"

"There's a complaint filed by a John Smith which was nonprocessed at the request of the FBI."

"FBI? Who in the FBI? Does it have an agent's name?"

"No."

"What about John Smith? Is there an address or phone number?"

"Nothing here," Potts said. "Let me see what I can find out."

Cerreta heard the tapping of computer keys.

"Oh, Christ, have you any idea how many John Smiths there are? They're marching across my screen now like ants running to sugar. There's no way I'm going to be able to isolate your man."

"Okay, Sarah, thanks," Cerreta said.

While Cerreta was on the phone, Logan picked up a sheet of paper containing all the information they had on Bart Eberwine and George Kinder, and began reading.

PRINCIPAL PROFILE: *Eberwine, Bartholomew W.*

Eberwine, age 34, has an MBA from Columbia University. He is a broker for the firm of Barry, Patmore and Daigh, with a yearly income, including bonuses, in the high six figures.

Eberwine is unmarried and is active in half a dozen civic and social organizations. He is very athletic, plays racquetball, tennis, and is an avid golfer. He also coaches Little League baseball. He has no police record.

PRINCIPAL PROFILE: *Kinder, George C.*

Kinder, age 33, had an MBA from the Olin School of Business, Washington University, in St. Louis. Kinder was a broker for the firm of Barry, Patmore and Daigh, with a yearly income, including bonuses, in the high six figures.

Kinder was divorced and had two children. He was active in several civic and social organizations. His hobbies were painting and collecting baseball cards. He was a good athlete, who played basketball in college and, more recently, in an amateur men's league. He was also an active racquetball player.

When Cerreta hung up, Logan looked up from his reading. "Anything?"

"I don't know, maybe," Cerreta replied. "But if there is, there's no way I can take advantage of it." He explained the nonspecified complaint filed by John Smith, as well as the notation that the complaint was nonprocessed at the request of the FBI.

"FBI, or IRS?"

"FBI," Cerreta replied. "Why would you suggest IRS?"

"With the kind of money this guy is pulling in, I would think the IRS would be especially interested in him."

"What kind of money?"

"High, and I mean very high, six figures," Logan said, holding up the confidential profile report.

Cerreta whistled. "And I wanted to be a cop." He sighed. "I guess I can put in a request, through channels, for the FBI to match Bart Eberwine with John Smith. They must have them linked in some way, or they wouldn't have asked that John Smith's complaint be nonprocessed."

"Through channels, huh? You know how long that will take?"

"Longer than we've got," Cerreta replied. "But I'm not going to just drop it right here. I can't."

"Didn't figure you would," Logan replied. "But we still got the runner to find. What about him? You have any ideas?"

"We could go talk to the parking lot attendant again," Cerreta suggested.

Logan shook his head. "It wouldn't be the same one. I asked yesterday. They alternate days."

"Yeah, well, that's not so bad," Cerreta said. "Perhaps talking to someone new will give us a new perspective."

"Maybe so," Logan agreed. Cerreta stood up to leave, and Logan held up his hand. "Hey, Phil, I could call Sally if you'd like."

"Sally?"

"Sally Bateman. She's a friend of mine who also happens to be a computer programmer for the FBI. Maybe she could run a check for you and put Eberwine and the mysterious John Smith together."

Cerreta smiled broadly. "You know, sometimes you're almost worth keeping around," he teased.

"The name is J. W. McKay, but ever'one just calls me Mac," the parking lot attendant at the Executive Stress Health Club said when Cerreta and Logan identified themselves.

"Mac, we'd like to ask you a few questions

about what happened yesterday, if you don't mind," Cerreta said.

"Me? No, I don't mind, but I don't know how I can help you. I didn't even work yesterday."

"I know," Cerreta said. "But you're one of the regular attendants here, aren't you?"

"Yeah. Well, we ain't like attendants exactly," McKay replied. "I mean, all the members here park their own cars."

"Do you know most of the members?"

"Yeah, sure. Well, I mean, not personally or nothin' like that. But I know 'em when I see 'em."

"Do you know Eberwine and Kinder?"

"Yeah, I know both of 'em. It's a shame it had to be Kinder. He was really a nice man."

"What do you mean? Are you saying you would rather it be Eberwine?"

"No, no, nothin' like that," McKay said quickly. "I mean, Mr. Eberwine, he's a nice guy too. But Kinder was a better tipper, you know?"

"Do you keep a pretty good eye on who comes and goes to the parking lot?" Logan asked.

"Yeah, sure, that's my job. We have to keep out the cars that don't belong," McKay answered.

"And the people?" Cerreta asked. "Do you keep them out as well?"

"Sort of. I mean, if I see anyone around the

cars that have no business bein' here, I run 'em off.''

"Do people often wander onto the lot who don't belong?"

"Kids do sometimes. We get some nice cars in here, you know? The kids like to look at 'em."

"But you keep them away."

"Yeah, sure. I mean, what if you owned a forty- or fifty-thousand-dollar car and some kid come around and scratched up the paint job. You'd be pissed, wouldn't you?"

"I'm sure I would," Cerreta agreed. "What about the two black guys who were on the lot yesterday? Do you think you may have ever seen them around here?"

At that moment a Volvo with a Missouri tag tried to turn into the parking lot.

"Excuse me," McKay said. "Hey, fella," he called to the driver. "Hey! Hey, you can't come in here."

"I'll pay," the driver of the car offered.

McKay shook his head. "This ain't no public parkin' lot. This here is a private lot for the Executive Stress Athletic Club."

"Do you know a parking lot near by?" the driver asked.

"What I look like? A information booth? All I know is, you can't park in here."

"There's a parking garage on the right-hand

side of the street about midway down the next block," Logan told the driver.

"Thanks," the driver of the Volvo said, backing out into the street again.

"I coulda told 'im that, I guess, but half the time they don't listen," McKay complained. "Now, where was we? Oh, yeah, we was talkin' about did I ever see the two guys that was in here yesterday. You mean the two black guys?"

"Yes, of course."

"Funny you would ask that, 'cause I think I did see them a couple days ago, talkin' to Tony."

"Tony? Who is Tony?"

"I don't know the last name. He's the guy has the pretzel cart down on the corner. I seen him arguin' with two black guys the other day, and I think it was the same two that was involved in the shootin'."

"Can you describe the two?" Logan asked.

"Late twenties or early thirties, I guess," McKay said. "One was a big man, over six feet tall, probably pushin' two hundred pounds. The other was shorter, not quite as heavy. Muscular, both of 'em."

"That sounds like them," Logan said.

"Yes, it does," Cerreta agreed. They started to leave, then Cerreta turned back to McKay. "I guess you walked out to the spot where it happened?"

"Yeah, jeez, I mean was I not supposed to?" McKay replied. "I was just curious, you know."

"That's all right," Cerreta said, holding up his hand. "I was just wondering if maybe you happened across something we may have missed yesterday. Like a switchblade knife?"

"No," McKay said. "Didn't see nothin' like that, but I'll keep my eyes open for you."

"Thanks," Cerreta said. "You've already been very helpful to us."

"You're askin' about the two black guys that was involved in that shootin' yesterday?" the vendor at the corner of East Fifty-seventh and Third Avenue said, replying to Logan's question.

"Yes."

"I didn't see nothin'."

"You were here, weren't you?"

"I'm here ever' day, from eight till five, just like goin' to an office."

"And you didn't see or hear anything?"

"I didn't say that," Tony said. "I said I didn't see nothin'. But I did hear the shootin'."

"When you heard the shooting, did you look around?" Logan asked.

"Just long enough to make sure that whoever it was, wasn't shootin' at me," Tony replied. A black Lincoln slid to a stop, and without asking, Tony put brown mustard on a pretzel, folded it in a wrapper, then passed it through the window. He took the money, made change from his apron pocket, then nodded. "Don't you worry none, Mr. Sadler," he called to the driver. "The Mets will come back tonight."

"They better," the driver's muffled voice replied. "They cost me a C-note last night."

Tony returned to his cart, and the Lincoln moved back into traffic. "He's a big Mets fan," he explained.

"Did you see the man who ran?" Cerreta asked.

"Yeah, I seen 'im. I told you, I looked up to see if anyone was shootin' at me. That's when I seen him."

"Did you see which way he went?"

Tony shook his head. "Not really," he said. "Soon as he turned the corner, I lost him."

"The parking lot attendant said he saw you talking to the same two men the other day. Did you recognize the one who ran as someone you had talked to?"

"Yeah, I talked to him the other day, him and the guy that was shot."

"What did you talk about?"

"Same thing I talk to most people about. They bought a pretzel."

"Do you know either of their names?" Logan asked.

Tony shook his head. "Sorry," he said.

Cerreta heard their call on the radio and he walked over to the car and reached through the open window for the microphone.

"Go ahead," he said.

"We have a positive ID on the John Doe. His name is Clarence Ellis, 1420 Adam Clayton Powell Boulevard. Do you copy?"

"That is Clarence Ellis, 1420 Adam Clayton Powell?" Cerreta repeated.

"Affirmative."

"Okay, I've got it. Thanks, we'll follow up." Cerreta put the mike back on the hook, then walked back over to the vendor's cart.

"Tony remembered something," Logan said.

"Yeah? What did he remember?"

"Yeah, well I don't know if it's worth anything," Tony said. "But I'm pretty sure I saw them same two guys talkin' to Fast Eddie last week."

"Who is Fast Eddie?" Cerreta asked.

"I don't know his real name," Tony explained, "but I see him around all the time."

"See him around where?"

"He comes around here sometimes. Most of the time, though, he hangs out over on Lexington Avenue. That's where his girls work."

"His girls?"

"Yeah, he's a pimp."

"What does he look like?"

Tony laughed. "Are you kiddin'? You can't

miss the son of a bitch, he dresses like a damn clown and he drives a purple Cad with a big, gold grill and gold wire wheels."

"Thanks," Cerreta said.

"Hey, you want a pretzel?"

"No thanks, they give me heartburn," Cerreta answered.

"I'll take one," Logan said, pulling out his money.

"I guess that means I drive," Cerreta said as they returned to the car.

"Yeah, thanks. By the way, what was the radio call?"

"We've got a make on our John Doe," Cerreta said. "His name is Clarence Ellis, last known address is 1420 Adam Clayton Powell."

Logan took a bite of his pretzel, then wiped mustard from his chin. "I'm glad we have an ID. That'll make it easier when we talk to Fast Eddie."

"Hey, there's our man down there!" Cerreta said a few moments later. "See him? He's on the corner of Forty-second."

"You sure?"

"Of course I'm sure. How many purple Eldorados with gold grills can there be?"

"Probably a couple of dozen on Lenox alone," Logan replied.

"Yeah, well, we're not on Lenox, we're on

Lexington, and that's him," Cerreta insisted. "I can feel it."

The driver of the purple Eldorado was standing beside his car, leaning against the door, talking to three women. The women were wearing extremely short skirts, dark hose, and spiked shoes. One of the women was black and the other two were white, but all three had very blond hair.

The driver was, if anything, even more done-up than the women. He was wearing a lemon-yellow jumpsuit and a broad-brimmed white hat. The pant legs of the jumpsuit were stuck down into knee-high boots, and the boots glistened with silver spangles.

Logan put the light on top of the car as they pulled to a stop behind the Eldorado. The three women, seeing the cop car stop, turned and ran. The driver started to get into his car.

"Stay right there," Cerreta said.

"Hey, man, what the fuck is this?" the driver replied, putting his hands on the top of his car and automatically assuming the spread position. "It against the law to stop and talk to women or somethin'?"

"That depends on what you were talking about," Cerreta said. Since Fast Eddie had assumed the spread position, Cerreta obliged him by frisking him. "Okay, Fast Eddie, you can stand up."

"Hey, man, only my friends call me Fast Eddie. You can call me Mr. Turner."

"Sure, if you insist," Cerreta said. He chuckled. At least he knew now that he was talking to the right man.

"You goddamn right I insist. I got a right to some dignity without gettin' shoved around by the police. What is this anyway? What you want with me?"

"Isn't that obvious? Look at yourself, at this car. You're a pimp, Turner, and those girls you were talking to don't sell Girl Scout cookies. We can take you in for pandering."

Fast Eddie laughed. "Man, you think I started this business yesterday? There ain't no law against dressin' nice, or drivin' a nice car, or talkin' to pretty women. You got nothin' on me."

"That's not what the girl says," Cerreta said.

"Girl? What girl?"

"La Tonia," Cerreta said.

"La Tonia? I ain't got nobody named La Tonia workin' for me."

Cerreta smiled. "What difference does that make?"

"What do you mean what difference does it make? You can't get somethin' on me from somebody I don't even know."

"Maybe not, but we can bring you in for questioning. Then we'll check out Crystal's story, then Sasha's story."

"Crystal? Sasha? Who the fuck are they, man? Where'd you get those names?"

"Same place I got La Tonia's name," Cerreta answered.

"You crazy? I don't know any women by those names."

"Like I said, Mr. Turner, it doesn't make any difference," Cerreta replied. "I'm going to cause you some grief, and it's going to cost you an awful lot of business while I run down these girls' accusations, one at a time."

"Man, what are you doin'?" Fast Eddie complained. "You goin' to get me all screwed up here."

"Maybe," Cerreta agreed. "Or maybe we can work something out."

Fast Eddie looked at Cerreta and Logan for a long moment, then let out a sigh of frustration. "Damn," he said. "Damn, I shoulda known. This a shakedown, ain't it?"

"You might say that," Cerreta admitted.

"All right, how much it goin' to cost?" Fast Eddie stuck his hand down into his pocket and pulled out a fat roll of money. The top several bills were in denominations of $100. Fast Eddie licked his thumb and forefinger and peeled off five $100 bills, then held them out. "This enough?" he asked.

Cerreta shook his head. "I'm afraid not."

"Come on, man, what you want?" Fast Eddie asked. "You can't be killin' the goose that lay the golden egg, you know what I mean? Take the goddamn nickel, man."

Cerreta waved his hand. "We don't want money."

"You don't want money? What do you want? Girls?"

"A name."

"What kind of name?"

"You were seen talking to Clarence Ellis and another man last week," Cerreta said. "We want to know the name of the man who was with Clarence."

"You want the name of the man with Clarence Ellis? Hell, I can't help you none. You see, I don't do much business with the brothers," Fast Eddie said. He smiled and waved his hand. "The people I deal with are white, come to the big city from Podunk, Nebraska, or some such place. They want to see the sights and get their wick dipped, and I'm in business to accommodate them. Most of the brothers don't need to buy it. So, what makes you think I was talkin' with Clarence?"

"What makes you think Clarence is a black man?" Cerreta asked.

"You said he was, man," Fast Eddie said.

"No, I didn't say anything like that. I just asked if you could remember talking to him."

Fast Eddie cleared his throat. "Well, it don't matter whether he was black or white, I don't remember talkin' to him, or the man you said was with him. What they look like?"

"You are correct in assuming that they are both black," Cerreta said. "Clarence is six-three, two hundred pounds," Cerreta said. "The other man is shorter, five feet, nine inches or so, and weighs about one seventy. He has yellow eyes."

"Yellow eyes?"

"Yes. Have you seen him?"

Fast Eddie shook his head. "I think I'd remember a brother with yellow eyes," he said. "I don't know nobody like that."

"If you get a sudden improvement in your memory, give us a call."

"Yeah, sure, you can count on it," Fast Eddie said, unconvincingly.

"Where to now?" Logan asked as they returned to the car.

"How about we try the address on Adam Clayton Powell and see if anyone remembers Clarence?"

"Sounds reasonable," Logan agreed.

Logan was leaning against the side of the car, watching as Cerreta stood on the steps, asking questions of a black woman. Logan was sure that the black woman was younger than she looked. Her face was drawn and haggard, her shoulders stooped from years of hard work, and yet despite all that, she had a sense of dignity about her, as if she asked for no quarter and gave none. She was holding a baby in her arms, and another little girl, not much older than the baby, stood with both her arms wrapped around her mother's leg. Two little boys, stair-stepped up by a year each, played on the stoop behind her.

In addition to the mother and her little ones, another half-dozen children, ranging in age from about three to about ten-years-old, stood around, watching. Logan had no idea if any of them also belonged to the woman Cerreta was questioning, though he assumed they were from other apartments in the neighborhood. Cerreta and Logan were the only white faces within a thirty-block area, and the large, curious eyes of the children underscored the rarity of the occasion.

"Don't know nobody by that name," the woman said after Cerreta explained who he was looking for.

"Thank you, ma'am," Cerreta said. "Sorry to have bothered you."

"Where was you last night?" the old woman asked.

"I beg your pardon?"

"Last night," the woman repeated. "They was a young boy died here last night. He died of an overdose, but that didn't keep the dopers from sellin' their drugs to our children. They sold drugs last night and they'll sell them tonight, right here on these steps, just like ever' other night. And you know why? 'Cause they know ain't no cop goin' come down here at night. You a policeman. You carryin' a gun, but you too scared come down here 'cept in the daytime. So what you think about us folks who have to live down here, nighttime and daytime? We can't leave. We stuck here with all the dopers and rapers and murderers."

"Yes, ma'am, well, we're trying to get all the dopers and rapers and murderers off the street," Cerreta said.

"You ain't tryin' hard enough," the woman complained.

Cerreta started to retort, then looked at this woman who had to live her life and raise her children in the middle of a battleground. He felt a tremendous sense of compassion for her circumstances, and frustration over the fact that there was nothing he, or anyone, could do for her or for people like her. He shrugged his shoulders.

"No, ma'am," he finally said. "Maybe we aren't."

"Nothing?" Logan asked as Cerreta returned to the car.

"Nothing," Cerreta said, opening the door and slipping in with a sigh. "Look around down here, Mike. You ever think what you'd do if you had to spend your whole life here?"

"I don't let myself think about it," Logan said.

"Yeah, that's probably best," Cerreta agreed.

"Where to now?" Logan asked, starting the car.

"I don't know. I feel like we're butting our heads against a concrete wall. We've spent half a day talking to the supers and longest-term residents in every building around here. Not one of them has ever heard of Clarence Ellis, or seen a man with yellow eyes."

"Do you think they're telling the truth?"

"Well, I don't necessarily get the idea they are lying," Cerreta said. "Though I can't imagine that talking to a white police officer is one of their favorite things to do."

"Any ideas?"

"The only thing I can think of is to take another look through the mug shots to see if we come up with anyone who matches the runner's description."

"Yeah, looking at mug shots has always been one of *my* favorite things," Logan said sarcastically.

Chapter
Three

"You found anything yet?" Cerreta asked. It was seven at night, and he and Logan were in the station house.

"No," his partner said. "Nothing." He pinched the bridge of his nose. "But to tell the truth, I've been looking at these mug shots for so long now that they're all beginning to look alike. I doubt I would recognize my own mother."

Cerreta chuckled. "What have you not told me, Mike? She's not likely to be in there, is she?" He looked at his watch. "What do you say we knock it off for a while and go grab a sandwich?"

"Yeah, I am kind of hungry. Come to think of

it, I've been hungry all afternoon. We didn't even eat lunch, did we?''

"I don't remember.''

"Seems to me like I read somewhere that it was a lot healthier if a person would eat balanced meals.''

"We're eating from the four basic food groups: hamburger, coffee, french fries, and doughnuts,'' Cerreta said. "What more do you want?''

"Pass the catsup," Logan said. "It's the closest I'm going to get to vegetables today.''

"Here,'' Cerreta said, handing over the bottle. He happened to glance up toward the television set mounted on a shelf in a corner of the restaurant. "Hey, look at that,'' he said, pointing. "Isn't that Eberwine?''

"Yeah,'' Logan said. "What is he, on some talk show?''

"That's *Perspectives*,'' Cerreta said. "Look who's on there with him. That's that kook from the Guardian Knights . . . what's his name?''

"Oliver,'' Logan said. "T. Goodbody Oliver.''

T. Goodbody Oliver was wearing a khaki uniform, complete with orange beret and orange tabs on the shoulder straps. On his collar points he wore silver oak leaves.

"Let's move down to the end of the counter

so we can hear what they're saying," Cerreta suggested.

"I'm not sure I want to," Logan replied. "I don't have the same fascination for that son of a bitch that you do." But despite his protestation, Logan picked up his hamburger and coffee and moved to the end of the counter.

"Tell me, Mr. Oliver," the talk show host began, but was interrupted.

"I prefer to be called Commander Oliver."

"That's a bit militaristic, isn't it?"

"I suppose it is," Oliver said. "But we're fighting a war, and wars are won by military organization. That's why the Guardian Knights are organized along military lines."

"Aren't you stretching matters a little to say we're fighting a war?"

"Not at all. Even the police admit it. Surely you heard Detective Sergeant Cerreta's remarks about revolution?"

"Ha! You're famous, Phil," Logan teased.

"Don't give me that shit," Cerreta grumbled.

"Be that as it may, Mister—that is, Commander Oliver," the host continued, "the military uniform, the insignia, all of this smacks of extremist groups, does it not? Nazis, Aryan Nation, that sort of thing?"

"I would like to quote a great American," Oliver said. "Extremism in the defense of freedom is no vice. And I resent the comparison to the Nazis and the Aryan Nation. Our group is not racially exclusive. We have African Americans, Jews, and Hispanics who are active Knights. And believe me, people who ride the subways, buses, or walk the dark streets are happy to see one of our patrols."

The host smiled. "You categorize Jews as a race, do you, Commander?"

"Yes. No. Well, you know what I mean."

"Yes, I'm sure I do," the host said pointedly. He turned to face his other guest. "Now, let's turn to Mr. Eberwine, shall we?" the host said. "Mr. Eberwine, you heard what Commander Oliver said about people being happy to see his Guardian Knight patrols. Would you have appreciated the arrival of a patrol of Guardian Knights? Or do you think they would have made the situation worse?"

"Two people were killed, I don't see how it could be worse," Eberwine replied. "Yes, I would have welcomed a patrol from the Guardian Knights. In fact, I would have welcomed anyone: Boy Scouts, Girl Scouts, the Long Island Bird Watching Society."

"And yet, when the chips were down, you reacted in a way that makes every decent citizen proud," Oliver interjected. "You stood up to the muggers, shooting one of them down and sending the other one running."

"That's true," the host said, regaining con-

trol of his show. "But unfortunately, your friend
—whom we can now identify as George Kinder,
a fellow executive in the investment firm where
you are employed—was killed, was he not?"

"Yes," Eberwine replied. "He was killed."

"So your intervention can't be qualified as
successful."

"Maybe not," Oliver said. "But there has to
be some degree of satisfaction in the fact that
the mugger who was killed was the same one
who killed George Kinder. Surely you can take
some heart, Mr. Eberwine, in knowing that by
your courage you have struck a blow for all New
Yorkers."

"By the way, Mr. Eberwine," the host said,
"for those of our viewers who aren't already
aware, perhaps you could explain how it was
that you were carrying a pistol."

"Yes," Eberwine said. "In my position with
the firm where I am employed, I am frequently
called upon to transport large sums of money.
Therefore I am licensed to carry a firearm during such activity. It just so happened that yesterday I made such a delivery shortly before going
to the health club for my regular weekly racquetball game. It was just a coincidence that I
had it with me."

"You're very fortunate that you are authorized to carry a weapon," Oliver said. "I have
filed the necessary paperwork for certain se-

lected officers of the Guardian Knights to be classified as private security guards, with the right to bear arms."

"I wasn't aware that the Guardian Knights were armed," the host said.

"We're not," Oliver said. "Not yet anyway. There are people who don't yet understand what we're about, and they're fighting us. In the meantime, our Knights go out on patrol, in constant danger of their lives. Our only consolation is that the average citizen is also prohibited from carrying arms, so we are in no more danger than they. I thank God that there are a few people around, like Bart Eberwine, who do carry weapons and who aren't afraid to use them when the chips are down."

"Do you think the average citizen should be allowed to carry a gun?" the host asked.

"Of course I do. It's one of the guarantees of the Constitution," Oliver replied. "Only now, the good guys are unarmed while the bad guys are packing Uzis, MAC-10s, and all sorts of heat."

"Yes, well, I'm sure our police would say that the fewer people—good guys or bad guys—who carry guns, the better off we all are."

"Yeah," Oliver growled. "And look how much good the police are doing us."

"We'll take that up after this commercial break," the host said, smiling at the camera.

"I've watched as much of that crap as I can take," Logan said. "I never thought I'd say it, but I'd rather look at mug shots than see any more of this."

"I've had enough of the mug shots too," Cerreta said, draining the remainder of his coffee. He glanced at his watch. "What do you say we pay Charley Doyle a visit?"

"Charley Doyle? You don't mean Lieutenant Doyle in Vice, do you?"

"Know anyone better to give us a line on a pimp?"

Logan smiled. "No. I don't guess I do. It's pretty late, though. You sure he'll be there?"

"Are you kidding? He'll be there. Charley and his vice squad are like bats—they don't even wake up until the sun goes down." Cerreta chuckled. "You ever met him?"

"Not really. I've seen him at meetings is all."

"You'll like him, he's an interesting character. Charley likes the sleaze. He's the kind of person that would hang around with whores, pimps, bookies, and winos anyway, so he may as well have a job where he can do it, get paid for it, and be on the right side of the law beside."

"Wait a minute," Logan said in the police station. "Before we go into the Vice squad room, I'll give Sally a call and see if she's found out anything."

"Thanks," Cerreta answered.

"You know you're wasting your time, though, don't you? If Eberwine had any dirt on him, it would be in all the papers and on all the TV shows by now. Once the media builds somebody up like that, they do their damnedest to tear them back down."

"Humor me," Cerreta said.

"Yeah, well, what do you think I'm— Hi, Sally. Found anything on our boy?" Logan pointed to another phone, and Cerreta picked it up so he could listen as well.

"What's all this about, Mike?" Sally said. "There's something going on here, and I can't figure out what it is."

"What makes you think something is going on?" Cerreta asked.

"Who's this?" Sally said, her voice rising in apprehension.

"Easy, babes, that's just Phil Cerreta, my partner," Logan explained.

"Oh . . . So you're the one that's gotten me into this mess."

"I guess so. And I want to thank you for your help. Why do you say something's going on?"

"They have your subject in an Access Denied file," Sally replied.

"Is that unusual?"

"Only to this degree," Sally explained. "I'm the programmer, I designed all the files and developed all the passwords. This one, however, is in a file that I didn't even know about . . . and none of the passwords that I know about will work."

"Damn," Cerreta said. "I knew it."

"Come on, Sally, I've never known you to let a little something like a denied access stop you. You can do something, can't you?" Logan asked hopefully. "Can you come into the file through the back door or something?"

"Oh, don't worry, I haven't given up yet," she replied. "I look at this now as a personal challenge. But let me tell you, you're going to owe me for this, Mike. And I don't mean a beer and a burger," she added in a throaty voice.

"You know me, darlin', nothin' but the best," Logan promised. "Didn't I take you to a fine dinner and a Broadway show the last time we went out?"

"And didn't I pay for my half?" Sally replied.

"Well, hey, don't blame me for that. That's a women's lib thing, you know that," Logan said defensively.

Sally laughed. "I'll keep working on it. Phil?"

"Yes."

"Do what you can to keep him out of trouble, will you?"

"I make no promises, but I'll try," Cerreta answered.

After they hung up, Cerreta said, "She sounds like a nice young lady."

"And you sound like my mother," Logan replied. " 'When are you going to settle down with a nice young lady?' "

Cerreta laughed. "It's worked well for me. By the way, you still think I'm barking up the wrong tree in going after Eberwine?"

"So, maybe our boy isn't as squeaky-clean as a hero should be," Logan agreed. "He's in a high-dollar business . . . maybe he got hooked up in some of those junk-bond deals or something. But even if he is, what does that matter? That doesn't relate to our case."

"Maybe it does and maybe it doesn't," Cerreta replied. "But I sure would like to find out why the FBI is interested in him." He sighed. "I hope Sally can come up with something for us."

"If there's something to be found, Sally will find it. She's got a hell of a lot more going for her than a pretty face."

"Yeah? Well, what does she see in you?" Cerreta teased. "What do you say we step into the vice-squad bay and talk to Doyle?"

The first thing to catch Cerreta and Logan's eyes when they stepped into the Vice squad room was a very attractive young woman whose beauty was somewhat distorted by an exceptionally heavy application of makeup. She was wearing a tube top over well-formed breasts, the protruding nipples of which gave away the fact that she was not wearing a bra. Below the tube top was an ultrashort leather skirt. She had one foot up on a chair, displaying a long, well-shaped leg. The leg was encased in a dark textured hose, held on by garters. Just above the garters a wide expanse of white thigh showed all the way to the hemline of her very brief, black panties. At this point on her leg the woman was strapping on a holster that held a snub-nosed .38.

"Careful you don't get too interested in your work and let him start feelin' you up, Marie," someone joked. "You might get to liking it so much that you forget what you're doin' and he'll grab your pistol." The others laughed.

"Honey, if I have hold of *his* pistol, he won't be thinking about mine," Marie answered in a throaty voice, and she made a grab with her hand to illustrate her point. The others laughed again, louder than before.

"Hey, Phil, what brings you down here?" a stocky, nearly bald man asked, smiling and extending his hand to Cerreta. "Come to catch the show?" He nodded toward the policewoman who was about to go out on an undercover operation.

"Why not? It's the best show going," Cerreta said. "Charley, this is my partner, Mike Logan."

"Logan," Doyle said, extending his hand.

' Logan shook his hand, then nodded toward the policewoman. "I hope she's a decoy and not just making a fashion statement."

Doyle laughed. "Yeah, how 'bout that? It's sure not like the old days, is it Phil? Then, the higher-ups thought decoy work was too dangerous for women, so we had to get men to dress in drag."

"I remember," Cerreta said. He laughed. "Every now and then we found someone who really liked it—not the decoy part, the dressing in drag."

They laughed again, then Doyle, who was now a lieutenant, invited them into his office.

"Nice," Cerreta said, looking around when they were inside. "Well, Charley, you've done all right for yourself in Vice."

"Yes, Vice has been vedy, vedy, good to me," Doyle said, doing a poor imitation of Garret Morris's Puerto Rican baseball-player character from the old *Saturday Night Live* program. "Now, what can I do for you?"

"Charley, do you know anything about a guy named Eddie Turner?"

"Fast Eddie Turner? Sure, I know him. He's a pimp, works midtown mostly. Generally has from ten to fifteen girls, half of them black, half of them white."

"I'd like you to do me a favor if you would," Cerreta said.

"Name it."

"I would like you to keep Fast Eddie under observation for a while. We're looking for someone who we have reason to believe is associated in some way with Fast Eddie."

"Who are you looking for?"

"We don't know his name," Logan said. "But we have a description."

"Let's hear the description."

"He's a black man, about five-nine, muscular, 175 pounds," Logan said. "He was last seen wearing khaki pants, tennis shoes, and a Georgetown Hoya tee shirt." Logan looked up from his little tablet. "And yellow eyes," he concluded.

"Yellow eyes?" Doyle chuckled. "You're talking about Teroy Brown."

"What?" Cerreta was surprised by Doyle's statement. "You know this guy?"

"Sure. Teroy Brown and Clarence Ellis. Find one, you find the other. They're Fast Eddie's slack men."

"Slack men? I don't understand the term."

"If one of his girls runs into a john who stiffs her, or gets rough with her, Fast Eddie sends Teroy and Clarence around to straighten him out. You know, to 'take up the slack'?"

"If you were guessing, where would you guess Teroy Brown might be?"

"I don't have to guess," Doyle said. "I know exactly where he is. He's at the Rack'm'up Pool Emporium on 138th Street, between Lenox and Adam Clayton Powell. Fast Eddie owns the building, and Teroy and Clarence spend most of their time there so Eddie can get hold of them when he needs them."

"Yeah, well not Clarence," Logan said.

"Him too," Doyle said. "Like I said, find Teroy, you find Clarence, or vice versa." Then, seeing the expression on Cerreta's face, he understood. "Wait a minute. The mugger who got popped by the citizen yesterday. Was that Clarence Ellis by any chance?"

"Yeah," Cerreta said. "You think that means Teroy will change his location?"

Doyle shook his head. "He hasn't moved. He was there this afternoon."

"Thanks, Charley, I owe you," Cerreta said. He looked at Logan. "Let's go pick him up."

"You have him in holding?" Captain Cragen asked. It was ten-thirty in the morning, the day following Cerreta and Logan's visit to Vice.

"Yeah," Cerreta answered. "Eberwine is on the way down to take a look."

"What about the other witnesses?" Cragen asked. "What was their name?"

"Bowers. I put a call in to the St. Moritz. That's where they're staying."

"Did you get through to them?"

"No, but I left a message."

"You're sure they haven't gone back to Illinois?"

"Indiana," Cerreta corrected. "No, they're still here. As a matter of fact, the desk clerk is holding tickets for them for a show tonight. He thinks they just went out for a while. As soon as they get back, I'll get them over here to look at a lineup. With Eberwine and the Bowers, we should have a positive ID. With any luck, we can close the books on it."

Cragen smiled. "Good work, Phil, Mike."

A uniformed policeman stuck his head through the doorway to the captain's office. "Cerreta, you wanted me to tell you when your Eberwine arrived? He's here."

"Okay, thanks, I'll be right there,"

"You have the decoys ready for the lineup?" Cragen asked.

"Everything's all ready, Captain," Cerreta assured him.

"All right, get your witnesses in there, get us a positive ID, and let's wrap this thing up. The quicker it's out of the public eye, the better off we are."

* * *

"I don't know," Eberwine finally said. He had been standing at the one-way glass for so long that the people in the lineup were beginning to get restless. "Maybe—Maybe number two."

"Number two, would you step forward please?" Cerreta said into the microphone.

All six men were black, but number two had the lightest complexion. He was also two inches taller than the others and about twenty pounds heavier. The extra twenty pounds was muscle; Cerreta knew that, because he knew number two. Number two was actually Sergeant Lorenzo Baker.

Sergeant Baker, who had been through lineups before, shuffled forward, then squinted as though trying to look through the mirror.

"Stand straight, number two."

Baker stood straight, then glared as if angry. It was all a game. The actual suspects were often belligerent. If Baker was just as belligerent, it would not make the suspect's belligerency stand out, thus ensuring a more positive ID.

"It may be number two," Eberwine said. "But I can't be sure."

"How can you not be sure, Mr. Eberwine? You were face-to-face with the two men who attacked you," Logan said in frustration. "You talked to them for several moments before the altercation occurred. Are you telling me now that you don't even know what he looked like?"

"I, uh, was more interested in the other one," Eberwine said. "He had a knife."

"*He* had a knife? In your statement you said both had knives."

"Well, I suppose they did," Eberwine stammered. "But the other one attacked me . . . this one ran."

"This one?"

"If it *is* this one," Eberwine amended. "I told you, I can't be sure."

"Step back, number two."

Sergeant Baker stepped back in line with the others. Now all six men, including Sergeant Baker and Teroy Brown, stared forward impassively.

"Take one more look," Cerreta suggested.

Eberwine stared at the men, then sighed and shrugged his shoulders. "I'm sorry. Like I said, it might be number two . . . but I wouldn't swear to it."

"That's just it, Mr. Eberwine. If you testify, then you'll have to swear on it."

"I couldn't possibly swear to it in court," Eberwine said. "I don't know if it was number two or not."

"Thank you, Mr. Eberwine," Cerreta said in barely concealed frustration. He leaned over to the microphone. "You may go," he said.

The six men in the lineup shuffled off the raised platform. They weren't going very far, Cerreta knew. Brown would be taken back to his holding cell, the others would hang around the station until the Bowers arrived.

"Will you be needing me anymore?" Eberwine asked.

Cerreta sighed. "That's all for now."

Eberwine started to leave, but turned back when he reached the door. "I wish I could give you a more positive ID," he said to the two detectives. "Believe me, no one wants these hoodlums off the street more than I."

"Yeah, so I've been hearing on all the talk shows," Cerreta said.

"You are sure they won't be able to see us?" Martha Bowers asked.

"No, ma'am. They're on the other side of a one-way mirror," Logan assured her. "Believe me, they won't see a thing."

"Well, I've seen such things in the movies and on TV, you understand," Martha said. "And I know that in the stories the criminals can't see the people who identify them. But those are just movies and television, after all. I wasn't sure if it was really that way or not."

"It's that way," Logan said. "You can see them, but they can't see you."

"All right then," Martha said, placated by

Logan's assurance. "Where do you want us to go?"

"Right this way, please."

The Bowers followed Logan into the viewing room and took a chair. Cerreta called the lineup back in, and even before they were in position, Martha spoke up.

"That's him," she said. "Number five. I would know him anywhere."

Number five was Teroy Brown.

Logan breathed a sigh of relief.

"You're sure about that?" Cerreta asked.

"Of course I'm sure. Look at his eyes," Martha said.

"Mr. Bowers?"

"Yeah, that's him all right," he said. "But just to be sure, I'd like to see his hands."

"His hands?"

"I told you he was about the size of a point guard?"

"Yes."

"Point guards have to handle the ball a lot, so I automatically look at their hands. The fellow who ran by us the other day was missing the tip end of his middle finger on his left hand."

Logan nodded at Cerreta. They had been present when Teroy Brown was booked and had noticed the missing fingertip during finger-printing.

"Number five, step forward, please."

Teroy Brown stepped ahead of the others and stood there, as dispassionately as he possibly could.

"Turn left," Cerreta said.

Brown did so.

"Turn all the way around, back to the right."

Again Brown responded.

"Hold both hands out toward the mirror, please, fingers spread wide and fully extended," Cerreta ordered.

Again, responding as mechanically as he had before, Teroy Brown stuck his hands out toward them. He opened them wide and spread his fingers.

"There it is," Ed Bowers said. "The missing fingertip. There is no doubt in my mind, this is the man who ran by us."

"I don't care what they say," Teroy said in the interrogation room. "I didn't do it. I wasn't there."

"We've got witnesses who swear that you were."

"We got two positive IDs in the lineup," Logan added.

"And there's the physical evidence," Cerreta said, bluffing.

"What physical evidence?"

"You shouldn't have touched the Dumpster,

Teroy," Cerreta said. "Your prints were all over it."

"Shit," Teroy said. "I want a lawyer."

"As we told you when we read you your rights, the court will appoint one for you."

"Fuck that," Teroy said. "I want my own lawyer."

"Robinette is here," Logan said. "He's in Cragen's office."

"Okay," Cerreta said. He closed the folder he had been working with and slipped it into the top drawer of his desk. "Let's go see where we stand."

Assistant District Attorney Paul Robinette was sitting in a chair in Cragen's office, drinking a cup of coffee. Robinette was young, intelligent, black, and ambitious. Any one of these things could sometimes cause a difficult working relationship, though in Robinette's case they were strengths. These strengths were why Ceretta and Logan liked working with him.

Robinette nodded a greeting when Cerreta and Logan came in. "Brown's lawyer is here," he informed them.

"Who did he get?"

"Willie Moore," Robinette answered.

"Willie Moore?" Logan said. "I thought that son of a bitch was disbarred."

"He was temporarily suspended," Robinette corrected. "He's back."

"Who is this Willie Moore?" Cerreta asked. "I don't think I know him."

"He's a damned ambulance chaser," Logan said derisively. "He used to hang around here all the time hustlin' work. That was before you moved over. He's a real slimeball who works right on the edge of the law."

Robinette chuckled. "Sometimes he goes over the edge. That's why he was suspended for a while."

"If you ask me, Brown would've done better with a court-appointed lawyer," Logan said.

"Not necessarily," Robinette replied. "People like Willie Moore can be very effective defense attorneys. They don't let a little thing like ethics get in their way, and you never know quite how far they'll be willing to go."

"Yeah, well, he can pull every trick out of the bag he wants with this case," Logan said. "It won't do him any good. This is a lock."

Robinette grinned ruefully. "Come on, Mike, you've been around long enough to know that nothing is a lock. With a little luck we'll get a full confession and be done with it."

"That would be best all around," Logan agreed. "Oh, by the way, did I miss something?" he asked Cerreta as they started toward the interrogation room. "You told Brown we had a match on his fingerprints. I didn't know that.''

''Yeah, well, we don't exactly have what you would call a match,'' Cerreta admitted. ''But there were some smudges that could have been his. I thought it was worth a bluff.''

Logan chuckled. ''It did get a rise out of him, didn't it? Are we going to have a problem with that?'' he asked Robinette.

''I don't think so, though it would probably be better not to mention the prints again,'' the assistant D.A. replied. ''If Moore picks up on it, you can say you were mistaken. We won't need them anyway. We have positive ID from the three eyewitnesses.''

''Only from two of the witnesses,'' Logan corrected. ''Eberwine didn't give us an ID.''

Robinette stopped walking, and when the other two continued on for a few steps without him, they stopped and looked back. Robinette was staring at them in surprise.

''Eberwine didn't identify Brown?''

''No,'' Logan said.

''Why not?''

''Maybe he didn't want to identify him,'' Cerreta suggested.

''You think he's frightened of Brown?''

''No.''

''Then why do you think he wouldn't ID him if he knew him?''

Logan chuckled. "You know Cerreta," he said. "He doesn't believe in easy cases."

"He may have a point. I'm not sure I believe in easy cases either," Robinette said. "Like this one. It would be a lot simpler if we had three positive IDs from the three witnesses."

"What if we don't?" Logan replied. "What difference does it make? The Bowerses not only identified him, they picked out a couple of features that pinpointed him. I mean, what about the yellow eyes and the missing tip of his finger?"

"That will certainly add credibility to their identification," Robinette admitted. "But the fact remains that Eberwine was not only much, much closer, he was also a principal. And if he can't, or won't, make a positive ID of our suspect, a clever lawyer like Willie Moore can use that to his advantage."

Teroy Brown's lawyer, Willie Moore, was a very pale, almost anemic-looking man with a bad toupee and nicotine-stained fingers. There were already four cigarette butts in the ashtray when the two detectives and the assistant D.A. entered the interrogation room, and Willie was lighting a sixth with the still-burning ember of the fifth.

"Where you been?" Moore asked. "I've been here almost an hour now. My time is valuable."

"Expensive, perhaps," Logan sneered. "Not valuable."

"Sarcasm does not become you, Detective," Moore said. "Mr. Robinette, could we please get down to business?"

"We're ready, Counselor," Robinette answered. He, Cerreta, and Logan sat down across the table from Brown and Moore. Robinette opened a folder. "Mr. Brown, we'll be charging you with murder in the second degree," he said.

"What? Wait a minute here! I didn't stick the man! Clarence did! Hell, even Eberwine will tell you that," Brown shouted.

Moore stuck his hand out to stop Brown from saying anything else, then he rested his forehead on his hand and shook his head with a sigh.

"Mr. Brown," he finally said. "If you are going to go to all the trouble and expense of hiring a lawyer, why not let your lawyer speak for you?" he asked in a low, frustrated voice.

"Well, then do somethin'," Brown said. "I told you none of this was supposed to happen. I mean, nobody ever said nothin' about a gun. None of it would've happened if that motherfucker hadn't started shootin' off his mouth. He started shootin' off his mouth and Clarence just went ape shit. You know what I mean? Clarence, man, he just went crazy."

"Is that your defense, Mr. Brown? That you had nothing to do with it?" Robinette asked. "That it was all Clarence Ellis?"

"Ain't just me sayin' that. Eberwine hisself done said it was Clarence what did the cuttin'. All you got to do is listen to what he say. You can't charge me with no murder. Anyhow, you a brother like me," he said to Robinette. "How can you work with the Man to bring one of your own kind down?"

"I am an officer of the court, Mr. Brown," Robinette said. "Color has absolutely nothing to do with it."

"You right about color havin' nothin' to do with you. You nothin' but a oreo."

"Wrong. I am a prosecutor."

"Yeah? Well, you prosecutin' the wrong man. I done told you, Clarence stabbed the dude, not me."

"Mr. Brown, I would like for you to understand that it doesn't matter whether you or Ellis stabbed George Kinder. You were equally engaged in felonious activity, and that makes you as much a principal as if the knife were actually in your hands."

"Not necessarily," Willie Moore replied. "A good argument could be made that this was little more than an innocent misunderstanding that got out of hand. The actual stabbing was a spontaneous action on the part of Clarence Ellis. Spontaneity means no premeditation, thus there is no way my client could know what Clarence Ellis was going to do. Without knowledge there is no conspiracy, and without conspiracy you have no case. You're looking at reckless endangerment . . . Man Two at best.''

Before Robinette could respond to Moore's argument, there was a knock on the door and Captain Cragen stuck his head in. "Phil, you want to step out here for a moment?" he asked.

"Sure," Cerreta said, excusing himself. As he left, the interrogation continued behind him.

"What's up, Captain?" Cerreta asked.

"Joanna Blaylock wants to talk to you," Cragen said.

"The TV reporter? Captain, come on, are you serious? You called me out of an interrogation to talk to that bimbo?"

"She says she has something very important to share with you about this case. When I asked her what it was, she said she would only tell you. She says she 'owes' you. I think you should talk to her . . . at least see what this is about."

"All right, I'll talk to her. Where is she?"

"She's in interrogation room three."

Cerreta started toward the room, then turned back with a smile. "One question, Captain. Am I interrogating her, or is she interrogating me?"

"I guess that's yet to be determined," Cragen replied with a chuckle.

As Cerreta approached the interrogation room, he looked over toward the one-way glass and was startled to see Joanna Blaylock's face staring out at him. Then he realized she only appeared to be staring, for from her side of the glass she was looking at what amounted to a mirror, and she was now busily primping, adjusting her hair, pursing her lips, and smoothing her eyebrows. Cerreta stopped in front of the window and looked at her.

"Baby, if you only knew," he said under his breath, chuckling at the scene.

The smile was still on his face when he stepped through the door and the newswoman turned away from the mirror to greet him.

"Well, Lieutenant, you're greeting me with a smile," she said. "That's a happy surprise."

"It's Sergeant, remember?" Cerreta corrected. "Captain Cragen said you wanted to talk to me."

"You do get to the point, don't you, Sergeant? Just the facts, ma'am?"

"Yes, ma'am," Cerreta said.

"Did you see yourself on TV?"

"No." It wasn't entirely a lie. He had seen only a videotape, not the actual show. But he didn't want to give her the satisfaction of knowing that he had.

"That's too bad. Our viewers thought you came across very well. You've been getting quite a bit of fan mail, you know."

"I heard about it," Cerreta said. "I didn't say those things."

"But of course you did, Sergeant," she replied easily. "I just edited out the bullshit and cut right to the core."

"Is that what you wanted to talk to me about? My TV appearance?" Cerreta asked. He put his hand on the door. "Because if it is—"

"No, Sergeant, wait!" Blaylock said. She picked up the large leather bag that served as her purse, then took out a videocassette. "I want to give you this. I think you'll find it very interesting."

"What is it? My TV appearance?"

"Hardly that," she answered. "What it is, my dear Detective Sergeant Cerreta, is a videotape which shows the incident you are currently investigating. It shows both the stabbing and the shooting."

"What?" Cerreta exploded, reaching for the tape. "Did you take these pictures? Have you been holding them back from us?"

Blaylock brushed back a fall of hair, then smiled wryly. "Well, you are quite welcome, Sergeant. We're always happy to help the police, especially when they show such gratitude."

"Where did you get this tape?" Cerreta asked.

"That's the trouble with you people," she said. "You're more interested in where the tape came from than in what's on it. For your information, and perhaps peace of mind, we did not shoot this tape. This came from the security camera in the parking lot."

"The security camera?" Cerreta said. "Yes! Damn, why didn't I think of it?"

"Don't feel badly, Sergeant, nobody thought about it," she said. "Security cameras have become so ubiquitous that people tend to put them out of their minds. They are no more intrusive to our consciousness than a flower pot or a lamp. And of course that's the desired effect. That way people will forget they're there and do all sorts of things in front of them . . . even murder."

"I do appreciate your bringing the tape," Cerreta said. "But I am curious as to how you got it."

"It was brought to us by an employee of the company that supplies and services the cameras and equipment, Eyewitness Incorporated," she explained. "He offered to sell it to the station for five thousand dollars."

"I'm curious. Did you buy it?"

"Not from him," she replied. "He doesn't own the rights."

Cerreta chuckled. "Excuse me? *The rights?*"

"Yes, the rights. Sergeant, you must be aware of the news, and subsequent commercial value of real-life events, captured on tape. You haven't forgotten the Rodney King incident already, have you?"

"I don't think that's something anyone is likely to forget," Cerreta said.

"Yes, well, companies such as Eyewitness Incorporated, who have their cameras strategically placed throughout the city, now routinely copyright their tape. Therefore, anything that one of their cameras captures becomes their property—the company's property, and not the property of the employee who discovers it. So, to answer your question, we are dealing with the company for the rights. We have not yet come to an agreement."

"I thought you said this was the film."

"We've already made copies," she said. "Until we get the right to show it, however, the copies are useless to us. You, however, do not have the same problem. This copy is yours to do with as you see fit."

"Why so generous, Miss Blaylock?"

"Sergeant Cerreta, this is my city too," she said. "I have a vested interest in seeing justice served. Besides," she added with a smile. "I treated you rather badly. I would sort of like to make it up to you."

"I appreciate it."

"I'm sure that you do. And I would like you to show that appreciation, Sergeant."

Cerreta questioned her statement with his eyes.

"Nothing sinister or underhanded," she said with a little laugh. "All I want is a little 'most favored reporter' treatment. If you have something that will be of interest to my viewers, and will not jeopardize your case, I'd like first shot at it."

Cerreta stroked his chin and studied her for a moment. She was a dazzling beauty, there was no denying that. But once a person could get around the fluff, they could appreciate Joanna Blaylock for the professional she was. Begrudgingly, he was even able to work up some admiration for her. Finally he smiled.

"For this case only, Miss Blaylock."

"Thank you, Sergeant," she said. "We have a deal."

"I'll walk you back to the front," Cerreta offered.

"Careful," she warned. "You might be accused of cavorting with the enemy."

"Let them take their best shot," Cerreta said.

The sight of Cerreta and Joanna Blaylock walking through the station, laughing and talking together, raised quite a few eyebrows. When he saw her through the front door and returned to the detective bay, there were dozens of questions hanging in the air, but he ignored all of them except the one from Cragen.

"What did she want?" the captain asked.

"To hand me a stick of dynamite," Cerreta replied. He held up a tape. "This is a VCR of the shooting and stabbing. Let's get Logan and Robinette in here and take a look at it."

When the tape was punched up, there was a second of dark snow on the screen, then color bars, then a message.

THIS TAPE IS THE EXCLUSIVE PROPERTY OF WACN-TV. ANY UNAUTHORIZED USE, COPYING, OR BROADCAST IS PROHIBITED BY LAW.

"I thought you said this tape came from the security camera," Cragen said.

"Yeah, it did. But WACN is negotiating to buy the rights, so I guess they're already putting their warning on it," Cerreta explained.

After the message left, the picture on the screen was of the Executive Stress Athletic Club parking lot. There were half a dozen cars in view, including the BMW belonging to George Kinder.

"How were we so lucky as to have the camera focused in the right place?" Logan asked.

"Actually, there are four cameras on the lot,"

Cerreta answered. "This just happens to be the camera focused on the vic's car."

"What's that? What's happening now?" Logan asked.

Though only the two black men were in the picture, it was obvious that one of them was talking to someone out of camera range. Actually, it looked like more than mere talk. From the way the person was waving his arms, and from the expression on his face, it could be interpreted as an angry confrontation.

"Hey, wait a minute!" Robinette said, leaning toward the table. "That's Brown, isn't it? That's Brown doing all the yelling."

"Yeah," Logan agreed. "Yeah, you're right, that is. And all this time he's been in there telling us that it was Ellis who was causing the trouble."

"Yeah, well Eberwine has been telling us the same thing," Cerreta reminded them.

By now Eberwine and Kinder had entered the picture, and it was obvious that the donnybrook was between Eberwine and Brown. Ellis and Kinder seemed to be holding back, watching, as Eberwine and Brown continued to shout at each other.

"I wish we had sound," Robinette said. "I'd like to hear what they're saying."

"Yeah, wouldn't that be nice?" Logan echoed.

Cerreta chuckled. "You ungrateful shits, I give you pictures, for chrissake, and you bitch because you don't have sound."

They let the tape continue to play. Kinder pulled out his billfold and extracted some money. He held the money out toward Teroy Brown, and, failing to get his attention, stepped up to him. There was a sudden movement on Brown's part, almost as if he were trying to push Kinder away. Kinder staggered back a couple of steps, holding his hands over his chest. He looked down at them, then fell.

At almost the same time, Eberwine took his pistol from the bag and pointed it, not at Brown, but at Ellis. There were two puffs of smoke and the gun in Eberwine's hand kicked up twice. Ellis went down and Brown turned to run. Eberwine watched him run for a few seconds, then raised his pistol as if he were going to shoot again. He held it for just a second, then lowered it. After that the tape went blank.

"Son of a bitch," Cerreta said as Captain Cragen punched off the tape player. "Brown is the cutter."

"Why would Eberwine tell us it was Ellis?" Logan asked.

"I guess that's a question we'll have to ask Eberwine," Cerreta said.

* * *

"Say, where the hell you guys been?" Moore asked when Cerreta, Logan, and Robinette returned to the interrogation room. "Figuring out that you don't have a case? Well, we'll make it easy for you. We'll plea reckless endangerment . . . save the state the time and cost of a trial."

"Nice try, Moore," Robinette replied. "But we're going for Murder Two."

"Murder Two? Are you crazy?"

"No," Robinette replied. He leaned back in his chair and crossed his arms on his chest as he stared at Brown and Moore. "Let's just say I'm packing the heat."

"Say, oreo, what the fuck you talkin' about?" Brown asked.

Robinette leaned forward and rested his arms on the table, clasping his hands together. "Mr. Brown, do you know that there are security cameras in the parking lot? There are several of them, in fact, pointing in all directions so that no part of the lot is uncovered. Smile, my friend. You're on *Candid Camera,*" Robinette joked.

"What? You got it on tape?"

"The whole thing," Robinette said. "And the tape shows, quite clearly, that it wasn't Ellis who killed Kinder. It was you."

"What is this?" Moore asked. "Mr. Brown, what is he talking about?"

"Uh, can I have a few moments alone with my lawyer?" Brown asked.

Robinette stood up and looked at his watch. "We'll give you thirty minutes," he said. "I can't stay here all day. One way or the other, we're going to get this case wrapped up today."

"Coffee?" Cerreta offered when the three men stepped out of the interrogation room.

"Sure," Robinette answered. "Why not?"

"Let's see if there's any left in the pot," Cerreta suggested, and the three men walked over to the table where a large Mr. Coffee coffee maker sat. Cerreta suspiciously examined the coffee left in the glass container, then poured three cups. "It looks pretty strong," he said. "For all I know, this may be left over from yesterday."

"Coffee is like chili," Logan observed. "The longer it sets, the better it gets."

"I wish I could share your confidence that we were about to get this thing wrapped up," Cerreta said to Robinette.

"That's just what I told Moore," Robinette replied.

"Wait a minute. Do you mean you don't think we're about to close the books?" Logan asked. "Damn, what more do we need? We've got everything on tape. All you have to do is show it to the jury."

"Juries have looked at videotape before and not believed their eyes," Robinette said.

"If you ask me, the tape has just opened up a bigger can of worms," Cerreta said.

"At least the mystery of what happened to the knife is solved," Logan suggested. "There was only one knife used, and Brown took it with him."

"Yeah," Cerreta said. "But that still leaves the mystery as to why Eberwine told us Ellis was the one with the knife. And why he claimed not to recognize Brown. As soon as we get through with Brown, I plan to get Mr. Eberwine down here. He's been on TV quite a bit lately. I want him to comment on this appearance."

"Well," Robinette said, looking at his watch, "the half hour is up. Let's see what they have to say."

"Mr. Robinette, perhaps there is some room for a plea bargain?" Moore suggested when they returned.

"If your client will plead guilty to Man One, saving the state the time and cost of a trial, I might be able to get the D.A. to go along with it," Robinette said.

Moore shook his head. "Man Two," he said.

"I don't think so."

"We're offering more than mere cooperation," Moore said.

Robinette looked puzzled, then leaned back in his chair and held his hands out questioningly. "More than mere cooperation? What more is there?"

"This wasn't a simple mugging," Moore said. "Clarence Ellis and my client were hired to do the job."

"You were hired to kill Kinder?" Robinette asked.

"We wasn't hired to kill nobody. We was s'posed to just scare 'em," Brown said.

"Who hired you?"

"Man Two?" Moore suggested.

Robinette drummed his fingers on the table for a moment, then nodded. "All right," he said. "If it's usable, Man Two."

"The man who hired my client was Edward Turner."

"Fast Eddie?" Logan asked.

"You know Mr. Turner?" Moore asked, smiling.

"Yeah, we know him."

"He is the other piece of this puzzle."

"You're telling us that Fast Eddie hired you to intercept Eberwine and Kinder?"

"Yeah," Teroy replied. "Listen, you don't believe me, you ask Heather, or Dawn, or Barbie."

"Who are they?"

"They're hookers, man. They work for Fast Eddie. They heard him tell us to do the two white dudes. They even saw him give us the nickel.''

''Why would Fast Eddie hire you to confront Eberwine and Kinder?'' Cerreta asked.

''I don't know. Maybe one of 'em owed him some money. Maybe one of 'em got rough with Fast Eddie's girls. He don't like it when people get rough with his girls. Anyhow, he don't never tell us why. He just tell us who, where, and when. Most of the time all you got to do is say a few words to the dude and that's all it takes to make 'em shit in their pants, you know what I mean? Sometimes they get down on their knees and start cryin' and beggin' us not to hurt 'em. Only this time this one dude, this Eberwine, he wasn't like that at all. That motherfucker wouldn't keep his fuckin' mouth shut. It's like he was darin' me to go on, you know? I can't be havin' nobody get away with nothin' like that. It get back somebody got away with somethin' like that, it's goin' make my job a lot harder next time I go out, you dig what I'm sayin'? So I got my knife out.''

''To kill Kinder?''

''No, man. I wasn't goin' do nothin' to Kinder. And I didn't figure to kill Eberwine either. All I was goin' to do was cut the mother-fucker up a little to teach him a lesson. I mean, I swear to you, man, I ain't never killed nobody before and I wasn't lookin' to kill nobody this time. But if I was goin' to kill somebody, it woulda been Eberwine and not Kinder.''

"How is it, then, that you killed Kinder?"

"That's the funny thing about it. I don't know how that happen. It was some sort of accident. I mean, I was goin' after Eberwine, you dig? Only the next thing I know, Kinder is in my face, man. He in my face wavin' this fuckin' money at me. I don't want nothin' to do with him, so I push 'im back . . . I mean that's all I meant to do, man, just push 'im back. Anyway, I push 'im back so I can get at Eberwine, an' I hear this kind of gurglin' sound. When I look over, I see Kinder holdin' his hands over his chest and there's blood runnin' through his fingers. I swear to you, man, that's the first time I knew I'd cut 'im. The next thing you know, Eberwine was shootin' Ellis. Then he say 'Get outta here.' My mama didn't raise no fool, so I got.''

"Wait a minute! Who told you to get out? Clarence?'' Cerreta asked.

"No, man, it was Eberwine tell me that. He say, 'Get outta here,' so I get.''

"That's a very interesting story, Mr. Brown,'' Robinette said. "If it's true.''

"It's true, man, I'll swear to it,'' Brown insisted.

"How about it, Mr. Robinette?'' Moore asked. "Do we have a deal?''

"All right, we'll go Man Two if your client will testify," Robinette offered.

"He'll testify," Moore promised.

After Teroy Brown and his lawyer left, Robinette looked over at Cerreta and Logan. "You two get hold of those three hookers," he said. "We're going to need some collaboration."

"What about Eberwine?" Cerreta asked.

"What about him?"

"Come on, Paul, there's no way he doesn't figure in this. I mean he lied about recognizing Brown, he even lied about who did the cutting. I want to show him this tape, then ask him some questions."

"I'll tell you what," Robinette offered. "We won't close the books until we've had a chance to investigate Eberwine thoroughly. But he isn't going anywhere yet . . . he's still playing the role of hero. Bring in the hookers first."

Chapter Four

Cerreta borrowed a car from Impound, with Kentucky plates. When he saw three girls hanging out at the corner in Times Square where Teroy told him they would be, he rolled down his window and waved. One of them, a hard-looking, leggy blonde wearing a very short, red-leather skirt, knee-high red-leather boots, and a white blouse, unbuttoned and tied just under bare breasts, walked over to the car. She put a practiced smile on her face, then leaned over.

"Are you looking for a date, honey?" she asked. At that moment she and Cerreta recognized each other. She had been one of the girls with Turner when Cerreta and Logan questioned him. "Oh, shit! A cop!" she said. She tried to jerk away from him, but Cerreta reached out and grabbed her arm.

"Hold it!" he shouted. "Right now, all I want to do is talk. Don't give me any problems and it won't get any worse."

The girl looked at him for a moment, then nodded. "All right," she said. "What do you want to talk about?"

Logan, who had been walking the street, came toward the car with the other two girls in tow.

"Get in the car," he said. "We'll talk downtown."

"I thought you said we weren't under arrest," the blonde said.

"You aren't, if you cooperate," Cerreta said. "Talk to us and we'll give you a walk. Now, get in the car."

"Cream?" Logan asked.

"Yeah, with lots of sugar," the leggy blonde replied. This was Barbie. The other white girl was Heather, the black girl was Dawn. Heather and Dawn took their coffee black.

"How old are you?" Logan asked Barbie.

"Twenty-three."

Logan raised his eyebrows in disbelief.

"Nineteen," she said. "I been in the life since I was seventeen," she added.

"Aren't you afraid of AIDS?"

"Look, don't give me no lectures, okay? I got a nice apartment, nice clothes, I go to shows, I even went to Europe last fall. You think I could make this much money working in a pants factory in Puxico, Missouri?"

"All right, girls, let's get down to it," Cerreta said. "I want you to tell me what you know about Teroy Brown and Clarence Ellis."

"Nothin'," Barbie answered.

"You speaking for all of them?" Cerreta asked. "Because if you are, you're putting yourself, and them, at risk of accessory to murder."

"What?" Barbie asked. "Where do you come off saying something like that?"

"We already have testimony that you overheard Turner giving Ellis and Brown instructions to kill Kinder. If you have knowledge of that, and don't share it with us, that makes you an accessory to murder."

"Hey, no way, man," Heather said. "Fast Eddie didn't say nothin' 'bout no killin'. He just told 'em to put a trick on 'em, know what I mean?"

"You'll testify to that?"

"Girl, you better watch your mouth," Dawn said. "You ain't bein' too smart."

"Oh?" Cerreta said. "She just got herself out of an accessory to murder charge. You two are still facing it. Now, who's smart and who's dumb?"

"I'm not facing no accessory to murder charge," Barbie said. "You want me to testify, I'll testify. But you won't like what I got to say."

"Why not?"

"'Cause Heather's right. Fast Eddie didn't say nothin' 'bout killin' anybody. He just said work 'em over a little."

"That leaves you," Cerreta said to Dawn. "You going down by yourself?"

Dawn glared at the other two, then shook her head. "No," she finally said. "I ain't goin' down by myself. What they say is true."

"Now, here comes the next question. Why did he send his muscle after those two men?"

"I don't know," Barbie said.

"You? You?" he asked Heather and Dawn, only to get the same answer.

"Were either of the men customers? Any of you ever see them before?"

All three girls answered no.

"All right, that's good enough," Cerreta said. "We'll have statements drawn up for you to sign. Oh . . ." He smiled. "And sign them with your real names, will you? Not your street names."

"After we sign, can we go?" Dawn asked.

"Yeah," Cerreta said. "I promised you a walk, you can go."

"We'd better not," Barbie suggested.

"What?" Heather and Dawn asked together. "Why not?"

"We go back now, Fast Eddie's goin' to wonder where we been. We better spend the night in the lockup."

"She's right, you know," Cerreta said. "I can fix it up with Vice to have a general sweep. You'll just be three who were caught."

"You promised us a walk," Dawn said.

"I'm not going back on my promise," Cerreta said. "Walk if you want to."

Dawn thought for a moment, then laughed, dryly. "This the shits, man. Never thought I'd ask to spend the night in lockup. Okay, let's go."

Cerreta couldn't resist adding, "You'll thank me for it in the morning."

What little hair District Attorney Adam Wentworth had remaining was still quite dark. He had a high forehead which went all the way back across the top of his head, and was prevented from being totally bald only by a ring of hair that circled his head from ear to ear. The lack of hair was not something he worried about or fretted over. It was a fact of life, and Wentworth's entire life had been built around analyzing, and then accepting, facts.

Wentworth turned off the VCR, then sat behind his desk and drummed his fingers for a moment. He looked up at two of his assistant D.A.'s, Paul Robinette and Ben Stone.

"That's a pretty damning piece of tape," he finally said.

"It was enough to get a confession out of Brown. And an offer to testify against Turner," Ben Stone said.

"For Man Two," Robinette added.

"Did you offer it to him?"

Robinette nodded. "I hope I haven't overstepped my bounds."

"No, that's all right," Wentworth said. "But there's something else about this case that's bothering me, and it's been bothering me from the very beginning. It's like trying to pick up quicksilver—the more aggressively you grab for it, the more it rolls out of your way. Every time I look at this case, I come up with more questions I want to ask. For example, why did Eberwine claim to have shot the man who stabbed his friend?"

"Maybe he just *wanted* to believe the person he shot was the one who did the killing," Stone suggested. "I mean, if he was unable to prevent his friend from being killed, maybe he needs the psychological reinforcement of thinking he at least avenged his friend's death."

Wentworth chuckled. "That's pretty good, Ben. Did you get that from Psych 101?"

"Probably," Ben agreed with a smile. "But do you have a better idea? Because if you do, believe me, I'm ready to listen."

"I don't have the foggiest notion," Wentworth admitted. "Your explanation sounds as plausible as any, I guess."

"I have to tell you, though, that Cerreta has had this guy Eberwine stuck in his craw from the very beginning," Robinette said.

"The guys working this case think there's more to it, do they?" Wentworth asked.

Robinette shook his head. "No, I think Cragen and Logan are pretty much ready to play the cards they've got. Cerreta is the one who is trying to make more out of it."

"Cerreta has been in harness a long time," Wentworth said. "When someone like that gets a hunch, I'm inclined to let him play it out. What does he want to do?"

"For starters, he wants to show Eberwine the tape."

"By all means, I think he *should* show Eberwine the tape," Wentworth agreed. "Do you have some reason why he shouldn't?"

Robinette shook his head no. "Not really. But we were already talking to Brown when the tape came in, so it seemed reasonable to show it to him first. Then, based on Brown's testimony, I thought we may as well go ahead and bring Fast Eddie in. I mean whether or not Eberwine told us the truth about specific details of the case doesn't seem all that important now that certain facts have been established. Teroy Brown, as seen on the tape, and by his own admission, is the man who stabbed George Kinder. Teroy Brown claims that he was hired by Fast Eddie Turner to confront, if not actually kill, Kinder and Eberwine. And three of Turner's girls have now provided corroborative testimony to that claim."

"I might add that all this checks out with what our investigators know about Turner," Stone offered. "According to Cerreta and Logan, Turner has been known to use Brown and Ellis as his muscle."

"Any idea why he sent his muscle after Kinder and Eberwine?" Wentworth asked. "Do you think it has anything to do with drugs?"

"That we don't know," Stone admitted. "We do know Kinder's autopsy showed no trace of drugs."

"Ellis?"

"He showed evidence of being a user, though no narcotic intoxication at the time of his death."

"There has to be some reason for this. Are Eberwine and Kinder clean? Any possibility they were dealers or gamblers? Did they consort with Turner's girls?"

Stone shook his head. "There's nothing to

suggest that they were ever with any of Turner's girls. And the idea that they would be dealing seems pretty unlikely," he said. "Both of them were making well over half a million dollars a year, neither was in debt, neither of them were gamblers . . . except for the stock market."

"Still, there has to be some reason why Turner sent his goons after them," Wentworth said. "I'm with Cerreta. I'd like to know if there is more to Eberwine than we've been able to discover." The D.A. leaned back in his chair and folded his arms across his chest. "All right, I'll go along with Man Two to Brown. Now, what do you have in mind for Turner?"

"I want to go for Murder Two, two counts."

Wentworth leaned forward. "Wait a minute. You're offering Man Two to the person who actually did the killing, admits it, and is caught in the act on videotape. But for Edward Turner, who was nowhere on the scene, you're going for *Murder* Two?"

"Yes," Robinette replied. "Turner hired Brown and Ellis to beat up Kinder and Eberwine. That is a felony. During the commission of that felony, two people died. In my book that leaves Turner culpable."

"You're going to have a tough job selling that to a jury."

"Maybe not," Stone suggested. "After all, Brown was just a soldier. Turner is the general.

To use the analogy of the press, we're at war with street violence. I would think the people would like to put one of the bad generals out of action."

Wentworth stroked his chin for a moment while he contemplated Stone's suggestion. Finally he nodded. "All right. We may be going way out on a limb, but let's try it."

"I'll call Cerreta and Logan and tell them to pick up Turner," Robinette offered.

Fast Eddie Turner was standing alongside his purple Eldorado talking to Barbie and Dawn when Cerreta and Logan squealed to a stop. For just a moment Fast Eddie wondered what was going on, then, when he saw both cops jump out of the car and move toward him quickly, he knew they were after him. He started to run, but since Logan and Cerreta had separated as they left the car to box him in, no matter which way he went, one of them would have him.

"Give it up, Turner!" Cerreta shouted, holding his gun in both hands, his arms extended in front of him. He was aiming squarely at Fast Eddie.

"Oh, man!" Fast Eddie said, putting his hands in the air. "What the fuck is this? I thought we already had our little talk."

Logan moved in behind Fast Eddie and

grabbed his arms, then brought them around behind him to put on the cuffs.

"Hey! Take it easy! What's going on?" Fast Eddie shouted angrily.

"You are under arrest for the murder of George Kinder," Logan said.

"Say what? Are you crazy?"

"You have the right to remain silent," Logan continued. "If you choose to waive that right and speak, anything you say can and will be used against you. You have the right to an attorney," he added. "If you cannot afford one and desire one, an attorney will be appointed for you."

"Man you don't have to read all that shit to me," Fast Eddie said. "I've heard it all before."

"I'll just bet you have," Cerreta said. He opened the back door of the police car and put his hand on top of Fast Eddie's head. "Get into the car, tough guy."

"Hey, what about my car?" Fast Eddie shouted. "I can't just leave it here."

"You won't be needing a car where you're going," Cerreta suggested.

Fast Eddie looked over at the two girls, who, by the fear on their faces and the pleading in their eyes, were hoping that Cerreta and Logan would show no recognition of them.

"Hey, baby," he called to Barbie. "Take care of my car. Take it back to the parking garage, and be careful with it, you understand? You scratch it up, I'm goin' to have your ass." Without missing a beat, he turned toward Logan. "What you talkin' about, murder? I ain't never killed no one."

"Maybe not," Logan said, "but your muscle did it for you."

"My muscle?"

"Clarence Ellis and Teroy Brown. You lied to us when you said you didn't know them, didn't you?"

"Yeah, man, well, maybe I do know 'em," Fast Eddie admitted. "But I didn't say nothin' about it 'cause I figured whatever trouble they was in was their own business. I don't know what you're talkin' about. I sure never told 'em to kill anybody."

"No, but you did tell them to rough somebody up, didn't you?"

"I ain't talkin' no more," Fast Eddie said. "I don't have to talk to you or to nobody. I want to see my lawyer."

"I think that's probably a wise move on your part," Cerreta replied as they drove off.

"We can forget about Turner going down easy," Captain Cragen said when Cerreta and Logan answered the summons to his office. Stone and Robinette were already there.

"What makes you say that?"

"Did you see who he called for his lawyer?" Stone asked.

"No," Cerreta answered.

"Aletha Hawthorne."

Cerreta raised his eyebrows. "Aletha Hawthorne? Hey, I know who she is. She's a pretty well-known person, isn't she? You always see her in the papers, on TV. Hasn't she testified before Congress a couple of times?"

"That's the one," Robinette said.

"Correct me if I'm wrong, but I wouldn't think Miss Hawthorne would come cheap," Cerreta observed.

"Yeah, well, what can I tell you? Mr. Turner is in a business that generates a high cash-flow."

"I don't get it," Logan said. "Why would someone like Aletha Hawthorne defend a low-life like Fast Eddie Turner?"

"Maybe she's doing it to keep in touch with the common folk," Cerreta suggested.

"You mean, to show that she isn't an uppity nigger?" Robinette asked.

"Well, I wouldn't say that," Cerreta replied uncomfortably.

Robinette chuckled. "Why not? That's what people sometimes think when an African American does something out of character, like earn people's respect and admiration, to say nothing of making a lot of money."

"Hey, what's out of character about black

people earning a lot of money and respect?"
Cerreta asked. "What about people like Michael Jordan, Darryl Strawberry, Michael Jack-
son?"

Robinette smiled. "That's a typical reaction,"
he said.

"What's typical?"

"It's all right for African Americans to earn
money and respect in the athletic or entertain-
ment field. But it makes people uncomfortable
if a black gets too successful in business, or law,
or politics."

"What people?"

"Hey, look, I'm not attacking whites on this
issue," Robinette said. "The truth is, it's our
own people who have the most trouble with this
sort of thing. But Aletha Hawthorne is one of
the rare exceptions. She doesn't have to defend
Fast Eddie Turner to maintain contact with the
people. Somehow she's managed to achieve
phenomenal success without losing contact
with her roots. She's quite a woman."

"Do you know her?" Cerreta asked. "I mean
other than professionally."

"Yes, I know her," Robinette said. "I'm not
exactly in her inner circle . . . or even her
outer circle," he added with a chuckle. "But I
do know her, and I have been an admirer of
hers for a long, long time. Ever since she came

to give a talk to the student body when I was still in high school."

"Didn't she run for Congress or something once?" Logan asked.

Robinette shook his head. "No."

"Are you sure?"

"I'm positive. If she had run, she would be in office now," he said. "She's been asked to run half a dozen times. She's always refused, though her refusals have been ambiguous enough to keep her on everyone's 'short list.' " Robinette stood up.

"Yeah, well, that just reinforces my point," Cerreta said. "Why would she defend someone like Fast Eddie?"

"Maybe you didn't read it, gentlemen, but according to the U.S. Constitution, everyone is entitled to a defense," Stone said. "Now, what do you say? Shall we go talk to Turner and his eminent barrister?"

There was quite a contrast between Fast Eddie's appearance and the appearance of his lawyer. Fast Eddie was still wearing the same plum-colored suit he had on when he was picked up. Only the jewelry was missing; the gold chains around his neck, the heavy bracelets, and the six rings. Those had been confiscated when he was booked, and put in a brown envelope to be held for him. The long, straightened hair and the perfectly manicured nails, however, were still a part of his overall image.

Aletha Hawthorne was wearing a plain, dark gray dress with no accoutrements. She was a short, blocky, very dark woman. There was nothing about her to set her apart from any other African American woman of her general age and build, until you looked in her eyes. They were absolutely kinetic.

Cerreta, Logan, Stone, and Robinette took seats on the opposite side of the table from the lawyer and her client.

"Hello, Ben," Hawthorne said, greeting Stone. She looked at Robinette. "And you're Paul Robinette, aren't you?"

"Yes ma'am," Robinette replied, nodding at her. Though he didn't show it, he was very pleased that she remembered his first name.

"Gentlemen, let's get down to business, shall we? The charge against my client is ridiculous," Hawthorne said.

"Not all that ridiculous," Stone countered. "Your client hired Clarence Ellis and Teroy Brown to beat up George Kinder and Bart Eberwine. While they were engaged in that hired activity, two men were killed."

"Nobody was supposed to get killed," Fast Eddie said.

"Nevertheless, someone *did* get killed," Stone replied. "Paying to have someone beaten up is a felony. And if the person happens to die during the commission of that felony, the result is murder."

"My client denies that he authorized any such assault," Hawthorne said.

"Miss Hawthorne, does your client deny knowing Clarence Ellis and Teroy Brown?" Stone asked.

She looked at Fast Eddie.

"I knew them," he admitted.

"And, do you also know Linda Mosby, Helen Peterson, and Karen Lucas?"

"Who? I don't know nobody like that."

"They are known to you, I believe, as Heather, Dawn, and Barbie."

Fast Eddie consulted with Aletha Hawthorne for a moment, then straightened up.

"Whether or not my client knows those women has no bearing on this case," Hawthorne said.

"Oh, but it does have a bearing on this case, Counselor," Stone answered. "Do you know them, Mr. Turner?"

Turner looked at his lawyer. "Don't lie," she told him. "If you know them, admit it."

"Yeah, I know them," he said.

"Do they work for you?"

"Maybe," Fast Eddie admitted.

"What is the nature of their work?"

"They are paid companions," Fast Eddie said.

"You mean prostitutes?"

Fast Eddie held up his hand. "I don't know nothin' about that," he said. "All I know is, sometimes a dude will want to see the sights of the city, you know what I mean? And he might figure that it's more fun to see the sights if he has a pretty girl on his arm. I put those dudes and the pretty girls together. Whatever they do once they're together, well, that's pretty much up to them. They're both adults, and sometimes things happen when a man and a woman is together long enough."

"By things happen, you mean they have sex?"

"I don't know whether they do or not," Fast Eddie insisted. "That's the part of it ain't none of my business. Like I said, man, all I do is provide the man with a good-lookin' woman companion to help him enjoy the city."

"You have a reputation for taking care of your girls, do you not, Mr. Turner?"

Fast Eddie smiled. "Yeah. I make sure they keep all their doctors' appointments. Good health is the most important thing we can have, you know."

"And if one of the men who uses the services of your girls gets a little rough, do you intervene?"

Aletha Hawthorne leaned over for a whispering conference with Fast Eddie. They spoke quietly for a few seconds, then Eddie nodded and straightened up.

"I make certain the man don't bother any of my girls anymore."

"Have you ever used Clarence Ellis or Teroy Brown in that capacity?"

"Yes," Fast Eddie said. He leaned forward and clasped his hands together, then smiled at Stone. "But all I ever told 'em to do was to go speak to the gentlemen in question and straighten 'em out."

"Go speak to them and straighten them out?" Stone asked. He leaned back in his chair and crossed his arms. "Come now, Mr. Turner. Do you expect me to believe that large, muscular, violent-prone men like Clarence Ellis and Teroy Brown would do nothing more than talk to someone to straighten them out?"

"That's it," Fast Eddie insisted.

"And is that what you told them to do with George Kinder and Bart Eberwine?"

"I don't know what you talkin' about."

"Mr. Turner, we have Teroy Brown's sworn testimony that you ordered him and Clarence Ellis to go to the parking lot of the Executive Stress Athletic Club to confront George Kinder and Bart Eberwine. And, Mr. Turner, we have corroborative testimony from the three girls you have just admitted work for you. Now, do you continue to deny it?''

''I sure didn't tell 'em to kill anybody,'' Fast Eddie said.

''What did you tell them?''

''Just like I said. I told them to talk to the dudes and straighten 'em out.''

''And now two men are dead as a result of action you initiated. Is that not right, Mr. Turner?''

''I didn't have nothin' to do with it.''

''Mr. Turner, by your own admission, you sent them to the Executive Stress Athletic Club to confront Kinder and Eberwine.''

''Yeah, I sent them,'' Fast Eddie admitted. ''To *talk* to them,'' he insisted. ''But whatever happened afterward wasn't none of my doin'. I wasn't even there!''

''Paul,'' Stone said. ''Would you educate our gaudily-dressed friend?''

''I'd be happy to,'' Robinette said. He opened a book to the bookmark, then looked up at Teroy. ''Mr. Turner, I'd like to read something to you. 'A principal is any person concerned in the commission of a crime whether present or absent and whether that person directly commits the offense, aids and abets in its commission, or directly or indirectly counsels or procures another to commit the crime.' ''

''What's all that mean?'' Fast Eddie asked.

"That means you had the knife in your hand, whether you were there or not."

"I don't need the Law of Principals read to me, Mr. Robinette," Aletha Hawthorne interjected. "I am well aware of the concept and its implications. Whatever happened between Clarence Ellis, Teroy Brown, and George Kinder and Bart Eberwine, has nothing at all to do with my client."

"Your client has admitted sending Ellis and Brown over there to 'straighten them out.'"

"And he has explained to you that by 'straighten them out,' he meant to talk to them."

"Well, they did a lot more than talk, Counselor," Stone said in an exasperated tone of voice. "Two men died as a result of that talk."

"Yes, I understand that two men died during that altercation. But you must understand that my client had nothing to do with that."

"How can you continue to say that, Miss Hawthorne?" Stone asked. "Your client *sent* them there, for chrissake! It was he who initiated the chain of events!"

"If I may suggest an analogy here?" Hawthorne proposed calmly. "Suppose you own a messenger service and you hire a driver to deliver packages for you. Suppose, also, that over the course of the day your driver, without your knowledge, begins drinking. Now let us say that your driver is involved in an accident while under the influence of alcohol, and he kills someone. The driver is guilty of vehicular manslaughter. Are you culpable?''

"That analogy has no place here, Miss Hawthorne,'' Stone said.

She smiled. "Oh, but I think it does. And what is more important, I believe the jury will think so as well. I'm afraid you have no case, Mr. Stone. No case at all.''

"Ah, but that's where you're wrong, Miss Hawthorne,'' Stone replied. "You see, in your analogy, the employer had no idea that his driver was drinking, therefore he did not know he was dangerous. In this case, however, Mr. Turner well knew the assault records of Mr. Brown and Mr. Ellis. In fact, we have records to show that he bailed them out on more than one occasion. It is ultimately going to boil down to your client's word against the word of our witnesses as to what he actually intended. We have four witnesses now, Counselor. I've no doubt that we can get more if we need them. You, on the other hand, no matter how hard you try, will never have more than Turner's word. Now, given the mood of the people to get the riffraff off the streets, do you doubt for one minute that we'll get the conviction?''

Hawthorne was quiet for a long moment,

then she sighed. "What will you offer for full cooperation?"

"Man One."

"This is incredible," she said, slapping her hand on the table and turning her head away in disgust. "You are charging the person who actually did the murder with Man Two, and the best you have to offer my client is Man One? How about reckless endangerment?"

Stone shook his head. "Teroy Brown had something to offer," he said.

"Yeah, well, suppose I have something to offer too?" Fast Eddie suggested.

"What could you possibly offer, Mr. Turner, other than cooperation?" Stone asked.

"Oh, you might be surprised, Mr. Stone," Fast Eddie said. "You see, this ain't at all what you think it is. It ain't got nothing at all to do with my ladies. There's another party involved."

"Another party?" Stone asked. He looked at Hawthorne. "Aletha, you know about this?"

Aletha held up her hand to keep her client from saying anything else. "This is news to me, Ben. Would you allow me a few moments with my client?"

"Fifteen minutes," Stone replied.

"Thank you."

* * *

When Stone and Robinette returned to the interrogation room fifteen minutes later, Aletha Hawthorne was sitting with her hands folded on the table before her.

"Are we ready to talk some more?" Stone asked.

"Reckless endangerment?" Hawthorne proposed.

"Man Two," Stone insisted.

She shook her head. "Reckless endangerment," she said again. "Trust me, Ben. I promise you, you will find this a *very* good bargain."

Stone studied her for a long moment. "All right, Aletha, let me hear who it is," he finally said. "If it's as good as you say, I'll deal."

Hawthorne nodded at Fast Eddie, and he began to speak.

"Bart Eberwine come to see me," he said. "He told me he wanted me to have Ellis and Brown show up at the parking lot."

"Wait a minute. Are you trying to tell me that one of the victims is responsible for his own mugging?"

"You got it, my man," Turner said. "That's exactly what I'm sayin'. Eberwine set this whole thing up his ownself. Only there wasn't s'posed to be nobody hurt. All was s'posed to happen was my two main men was s'posed to scare the shit out of the two white dudes."

"Do you know Bart Eberwine, Mr. Turner?" Stone asked.

"I never even see the motherfucker in my life before last week. And I wish to hell now I never see him at all."

"What was the occasion of your meeting?" Stone asked.

"It happened one day last week when I was parked down on East Fifty-seventh. This white, rich-lookin' dude come over to see me. I figure here's one of them privileged white shits wantin' a walk on the wild side. Only, 'stead of askin' me for a girl, he give me a envelope with five thousand dollars in it. I say, 'What this for?' He told me there'd be another five thousand if I'd do him this little favor. I hand the envelope back to him. 'Man, I ain't goin' kill nobody for you,' I say. 'Leastwise, not for this kind of money.' He push the envelope back and say, 'You don't have to kill nobody. All you gotta do is have some muscle come down to the parkin' lot of the Executive Stress Athletic Club at about three-thirty, Wednesday afternoon. I just want them there,' he say, 'that's all.' So I say, 'What they goin' do?' And he say, 'I don' want them to hurt nobody. I just want them to scare the shit out of me and a friend.' I say, 'You one crazy motherfucker, you know that? What all this about?' And he say, 'Don't ask no questions. Just take your money and do what I tell you.' "

"So you sent Brown and Ellis down to the parking lot?" Stone said.

Fast Eddie nodded his head. "At three-thirty on Wednesday, just like Eberwine say."

"What did you tell them?"

"I didn't tell 'em nothin'," Turner said. "I don't never tell 'em nothin'. I just tell 'em where to go. They know what to do, so they do the rest."

"You didn't tell them that this was a 'special' arrangement?"

"No. I figure if they know too much, they goin' want more than the five hunnert dollars I usually give 'em. But I swear to you, man, there weren't nobody s'posed to get killed. Didn't nobody say nothin' 'bout nobody gettin' killed."

Stone drummed his fingers for a long moment as he contemplated the offer. Finally he sighed. "All right, Miss Hawthorne," he said. "You have a deal."

"I told you, never underestimate a veteran's gut instinct," Wentworth said after hearing Stone and Robinette's report in his office. "It looks like Cerreta was right about Eberwine all along. I'll go along with the plea bargain on Turner, but what about Eberwine? Where is he now?"

"Captain Cragen sent Cerreta and Logan to bring him in," Stone said.

Wentworth smiled. "I'll just bet that wasn't an order he had to give twice."

Chapter Five

"I'm glad you picked me up," Eberwine said in the interrogation room. "No, really I am," he added when he saw the expression on Cerreta's face. "I've actually been wanting to come forth from the very beginning to explain what happened, but things started getting away from me. You know, television, the newspapers, national magazines, I was a hero. I even got proposals through the mail, for chrissake, did you know that?" Eberwine shook his head in surprise. "The whole thing just sort of exploded. It was like riding the back of a tiger. I couldn't get off."

"You're off now," Logan said.

"Yes, I'm off now."

"Mr. Eberwine, you have had your rights explained to you, you understand that you have the right to remain silent, and you have the right to an attorney?" Cerreta asked him.

"I understand," Eberwine answered. "But I have nothing to hide. I am prepared to answer your questions without an attorney present."

"That might not be such a good idea," Logan suggested.

"No, it's all right," Eberwine replied. "I told you, I want to make a clean sweep of it."

Cerreta and Logan looked at each other in surprise, then Cerreta shrugged and began the questioning.

"Do you admit to hiring Brown and Ellis?"

"Yes, I admit it," Eberwine said. "Well, not Brown and Ellis. I never saw them before the day all this happened. But I did make arrangements with Turner to have someone, uh, show up at the athletic club. But not to kill anyone," he added quickly. "I certainly never intended for that to happen."

"What, exactly, did you intend to happen?" Cerreta asked.

Eberwine ran his hand through his hair and sighed. "As I look back upon it now, I find it almost impossible to reconstruct the reasoning process that led me into this . . . this tragedy," he said. "But I will try and explain, perhaps as much to myself as to you, what happened, and why." He was quiet for a moment. "You see, I wanted George's gratitude," he said.

"You wanted his gratitude? So you hired a couple of thugs to beat him up?"

"No, no, nothing like that," Eberwine replied. "Actually, nothing physical was ever supposed to take place. The arrangement was that Turner would send a couple of men down to begin harassing us. I would then pull the gun out of my bag and run them off. They understood—that is, I thought they understood—that nothing would actually happen. You can imagine my surprise, then, when they didn't run off . . . when the one fellow—Ellis, I think you said—stabbed poor George."

"That brings up another point, Mr. Eberwine," Cerreta said. "It wasn't Ellis who stabbed Kinder. It was Brown."

"Ellis, Brown, I get their names confused."

"No, sir, you have confused more than their names," Cerreta said. "You see, the man you shot is not the one who stabbed Kinder. The one who stabbed Kinder is the one who got away."

"No. No, that's not true. The man I shot is the one who stabbed poor George."

"Oh but it *is* true, Mr. Eberwine," Cerreta said. "You see, we have the whole thing on tape."

"On tape?"

"The security camera at the parking lot caught the whole thing," Logan said. "Would you care to see it?"

"Yes. Yes, I would like very much to see it," Eberwine replied.

"I'll go get the machine and get it set up," Logan said.

"Was George Kinder gay, Mr. Eberwine?" Cerreta asked while Logan was gone.

"What? No, of course not. Why would you ask such a thing? Why, he had a wife and children."

"An ex-wife," Cerreta said. He shrugged. "Sometimes it happens. Someone who is gay will try and live a straight life, then find that he can't do it. Even after they've married and had kids."

"George Kinder was no more gay than I am," Eberwine said.

"Funny you should bring that up," Cerreta replied. "That was my next question. Are you gay?"

"No, I most definitely am not! Why are you asking such a thing?"

"You said you wanted to get Kinder's gratitude. Sometimes that's the kind of thing a man will do when he's trying to win a sexual favor from someone."

Eberwine laughed dryly. "Sergeant, I am amused by the rather convoluted leap in your logic.'' The smile left his face. ''Though my own logic was just as faulted . . . and with much more tragic results.'' He sighed. ''No, Sergeant, I must confess to be driven more by avarice than by any sexual desire. I wanted to curry his favor for business reasons,'' he explained. ''You see, I was trying to put together an investment package that George had some reservations about. I thought if I could win his gratitude, he would withdraw his objections.''

''Did he have the authority to disapprove your investment package?''

''No, not directly,'' Eberwine answered. ''But it was going to be difficult enough to sell the idea to the firm. And I was afraid that if George raised his own reservations about it, the deal would be impossible to put through.''

''Why would Kinder resist?''

''You have to understand the difference in our philosophies. I'm somewhat of a free-swinging wheeler-dealer. George, on the other hand, is much more . . . was much more,'' he corrected himself, ''conservative. I used to tease him that his conservatism was the product of his midwestern background. And, to be honest, in its place, a certain degree of conservatism is a good thing, especially recently, in light of such things as the Lincoln Savings and Loan scandal and the Ivan Boesky affair. But rock-solid conservatism can also be inhibiting. And in these troubled times there is the occasional need for calculated risk if that risk can be justified by the reward to be gained. The plan I was working on could have tremendous rewards for the company if it was successful . . . but it did entail a good deal of risk. George was, I felt, overly concerned about the risk."

"And you thought that having someone threaten to beat him up would change his mind?"

"You have entirely missed the point, Sergeant Cerreta," Eberwine said. "I have already explained to you, I had no intention of it going as far as it did. I fully intended to stop it before the first blow was struck. All that was supposed to happen was a little posturing and intimidating language. I was then going to step in and put a halt to it. The two men, Ellis and Brown, would run away, and George would be forever grateful."

"That's a pretty farfetched plan, isn't it?"

"Yes," Eberwine admitted. "It is. But as I said, I had no idea it would get out of hand."

The door to the interrogation room opened at that moment and Logan stepped in with a combination TV and VCR unit. He plugged the set in, then slipped the videocassette into the slot.

* * *

For a long moment after the tape was shown, Eberwine sat at the table with his forehead in his hand.

"Mr. Eberwine?" Cerreta finally said. "You don't deny that was you on the tape, do you?"

"No," Eberwine finally said. "I don't deny it. But I don't understand. I would have sworn that the man I shot was the one who stabbed George."

"Mr. Eberwine, when you were shown Teroy Brown in the lineup, why didn't you identify him?" Logan asked.

"I don't know. I truly didn't recognize him. So, what happens now?" Eberwine asked.

"What happens now, Mr. Eberwine, is that we book you," Cerreta replied. "You are under arrest for the wrongful deaths of George Kinder and Clarence Ellis."

Eberwine gasped. "What do you mean for Clarence Ellis *and* George Kinder? How can you do that? I mean, I admit to shooting Ellis in self-defense, but how does poor George fit into the picture? You can't be serious."

"I assure you, sir, we are very serious," Cerreta said.

"In that case, gentlemen, I think it would be in my best interest to say nothing more until I have an attorney present."

"Mr. Eberwine, I think that would be a prudent move on your part," Cerreta agreed.

Cerreta stood up, then looked over at Eberwine. Even now, he was smooth, slick, and unruffled. Cerreta felt an itch in the palm of his hands, and he wished he could reach across the table and grab Eberwine by his smug neck. He couldn't do that, of course, but it was pleasurable to think about it.

Then Cerreta smiled, because he knew what would ruffle the man's feathers. A smooth operator like Bart Eberwine would not like the unfavorable publicity an indictment would bring. And he did owe Johanna Blaylock a favor.

"Stay with our friend for a moment, would you?" he asked Logan. "There's something I need to do."

Cerreta returned to his desk, then called the TV station to ask for Blaylock.

"May I tell her what this is about?"

"No," Cerreta growled. "Just tell her it's Detective Cerreta. She'll either talk to me or she won't."

"One moment, sir."

Less than half a minute later Cerreta heard her voice. "Of course I'll talk to you," she said. "Do you have something for me?"

"Yeah, I do," Cerreta replied. "We're arresting Wyatt Earp."

"Wyatt Earp?" she said, confused, then she took in a quick gasp. "You're talking about

Eberwine? Bart Eberwine? But I thought—" she began, only to be cut off by Cerreta.

"Yeah, that's what everyone thought. It'll be in all the papers tomorrow. If you want it now, get down here."

"I'm on my way," Blaylock said.

New York *Post*

FROM HERO TO VILLAIN
EBERWINE TO BE ARRAIGNED TODAY

New York Times

WALL STREET BROKER ARRESTED, INDICTED

Just before the judge came in, one of the court bailiffs walked over to the defense table and handed a book to one of the men sitting there.

"Mr. Henry, would you autograph this for me?" he asked.

Tom Henry, attorney for the defense, was tall and well-proportioned. His dark brown hair had an auburn hue, and there were distinguished tufts of gray appearing at his temples. He smiled broadly and his eyes flashed in amusement as he took the book from the bailiff.

"You the Jury," he said, reading the title. He

laughed. "Of course, that is with apologies to Mickey Spillane. By the way, did you enjoy it?"

The bailiff smiled in embarrassment. "Actually, I haven't read it," he admitted. "But my wife did, and she thought it was great."

"Well, perhaps I should autograph it to her," Henry suggested.

"Would you? She would be thrilled, I know she would. Her name is Alice."

Tom Henry scribbled his name in the book, then handed it back to the bailiff.

"That's all we need," Stone whispered to Robinette. "Tom Henry has his fan club here, rooting for him."

"Did you read the book?" Robinette asked. "It was pretty good."

Stone chuckled. "Come on, Paul, don't tell me you're star-struck too."

"Not star-struck exactly," Robinette answered. "But it is a good book."

The judge, a thin, gray-haired woman, came into the courtroom then and took her place on the bench. She shuffled through a few papers, obviously looking for something, then called over a clerk. He pointed out the correct paper and she nodded, then cleared her throat.

"The charges are manslaughter in the second degree, and reckless endangerment," Judge Margaret Allen intoned. "How does the defendant plead?"

Henry whispered something to Eberwine, who then stood and said: "Not guilty, Your Honor."

"Bail recommendation, Mr. Stone?"

"Five hundred thousand dollars, Your Honor," Stone said.

"You have a reason, I'm sure, for requesting such a high bail?" Judge Allen asked.

"Mr. Eberwine is a man of considerable means. If the bail is not high enough to get his attention, I'm afraid it will have little effect."

Tom Henry stood up and brushed a fall of hair back from his forehead. "Your Honor, my client *is* a man of considerable means, that is true. But it is that very thing that will prevent him from running away. He is a lifelong resident of the city of New York, heavily invested here both financially and emotionally. He is not a risk to flee. Request that he be released on his own recognizance."

"He may have a personal investment in New York, Mr. Henry, but this isn't a speeding ticket. Your client has been indicted for manslaughter. Bail is set for $250,000. Trial date is," the judge looked at her calendar, "August tenth." She rapped her gavel to conclude the hearings.

Stone and Robinette were in the hall just outside when a smiling Tom Henry stepped up to them. He stuck his hand out toward Robinette.

"Paul Robinette, isn't it?" he asked.

"Yes," Robinette answered.

"I know some of your work. Your summation on the Oscar Dagen case was extremely good."

"Thank you," Robinette said, smiling broadly at the flattery.

"If you ever get tired of working for twenty dollars and found, or whatever paltry sum the people pay, come see me. There's always room for a bright young lawyer who's on his way up."

"Thank you for the invitation, Counselor," Robinette said. "But I'm quite happy where I am."

"Yes, well, that's because our mutual friend Benjamin, here, has you brainwashed. That is true, isn't it, Ben? You have subjugated this young man's free will?"

"Paul is his own man, Counselor," Stone said.

"So you say. By the way, Ben, where have you been keeping yourself? I haven't seen you around at any of the social functions lately."

Stone smiled. "You say that, Tom, as if we actually ran in the same social set."

Henry made a tsking sound and shook his head. "Maybe it's because I can't understand why you don't," he replied. "After all, you were one of the brightest students in our class. We figured you would be right up there with the greats: Clarence Darrow, Melvin Belli, Percy

Forman, and Ben Stone. But instead of defending people, you chose to prosecute them."

"That I did, Tom, that I did."

"Such is the waste. You aren't having second thoughts now, are you?"

"Not at all," Stone replied. "I've never regretted a moment of it. You know me, Tom. I've always liked a challenge."

Henry chuckled. "Well, I'm glad you like a challenge, Ben, for you certainly have one in front of you now." He nodded toward Eberwine, who was at that moment talking to half a dozen reporters from both print and television. "To try and criminalize a tragic error in judgment is a task of no small undertaking. In truth, I'm amazed that the grand jury would hand down the indictment, even allowing for the fact that the grand jury system is in the D.A.'s pocket. You must have made a brilliant presentation."

"Oh, I did, Tom, I did," Stone said. "Too bad you couldn't have seen me."

"Isn't it?" Henry replied. "But of course, defense attorneys aren't allowed before grand juries, are they?" He wagged his finger and smiled. "However, we *are* allowed before the judge and jury. It is going to be interesting to see if your presentation is as . . . persuasive this time."

"Yes, it will be interesting, won't it?" Stone replied.

"You and Tom Henry were classmates in school?" Robinette asked in surprise, after Henry left.

Stone smiled. "We were more than mere classmates, my friend. We were debating partners on the college debating team."

"I'm impressed," Robinette said. "Thomas Henry is one of the most successful trial lawyers in the entire country. I can remember when I was still in school, watching him in the Brandenberg case. You remember Karl von Brandenberg? He was married to some big oil heiress and he was accused of murdering her. CNN carried the whole trial. Never mind that the case had all the elements that attract public attention: sex, money, and murder. It was, without doubt, the most brilliantly executed defense I ever saw. No wonder the guy is worth five hundred dollars an hour."

"How closely did you watch the case?" Stone asked.

"I watched as much of it as I could while keeping up my studies. I told you, I was still in school," Robinette said.

"Did you watch it closely enough to see who was at the prosecutor's table?"

Robinette's eyes grew wide. "You?" he asked. "You were the prosecutor?"

"I wasn't in charge of the prosecution, but I did assist."

"Oh," Robinette said. "I'm sorry."

"Hey, don't apologize," Stone said. "You're right, Tom was brilliant in that trial. But that was then and this is now. This time we'll beat him."

"Damn!" Robinette said, smiling broadly. "Can you imagine taking down Tom Henry? Wouldn't that be a notch worth putting in our belt?"

"Oh, I can more than imagine it, Paul. We're damn well going to do it."

"Hey, Cerreta," someone shouted when Cerreta came back from the arraignment. "There's some woman been trying to get hold of you this morning. Name's Sally."

"What's she calling you here for, Phil?" one of the other officers asked. "I distinctly heard you say the other day, 'Honey, never call me at home or the office.'"

Several of the other officers laughed.

"She leave a number?" Cerreta asked, not reacting to the teasing.

"Yeah, it's under your phone."

Cerreta dialed the number, then listened to the rings until Sally answered.

"Phil Cerreta," he said.

"Do you have any idea how many Smith's with the first or last name of John have had business with the FBI in the last five years?"

"How many?"

"You don't want to know," Sally answered. "Enough to keep me busy, that's for sure. Anyway, I think I have the information you want."

"You do?" Cerreta said excitedly. "Girl, I could kiss you."

"Promises, promises, that's all I ever get from married men," Sally replied. "What's your fax number?"

"It's 766-3576."

"Stand by," Sally said.

"What's that?" Logan asked a moment later, arriving just as the paper was working its way through the fax machine.

"John Smith," Cerreta replied.

Logan smiled broadly. "Sally found him?"

"Yep."

"Where?"

Cerreta looked at the paper. "In the Barry, Patmore and Daigh Building."

"Impossible, we went over every employee of the firm with a fine-tooth comb," Logan replied. "There were no John Smiths."

"He doesn't exactly work for the firm," Cerreta said. "He's what you might call an entrepreneur. He owns the sandwich, coffee, and doughnut concession for the entire building.''

"What was the nature of his complaint?"

"Manipulation of the market and financial improprieties," Cerreta said.

"Wait a minute, a sandwich vendor made those complaints? Isn't that a little out of his area?"

"It may be," Cerreta agreed. "But the FBI evidently took him seriously. They asked the city for a nonprocess of the complaint, then they put it in a locked file, so that Sally nearly didn't get to it."

"Maybe we'd better go talk to Mr. Smith," Logan said.

"You're sure we aren't just wasting our time?" Cerreta teased.

"Come on, Phil, you're too big a person for 'I told you so,' " Logan complained.

John Smith had a room just off the custodian's room in the basement of the Barry, Patmore, and Daigh Building. One wall of the room was lined with shelves stocked with bottles of catsup, mayonnaise, mustard, pickles, peppers, and various other condiments. Another wall was lined with stainless steel, commercial-type refrigerators. When Cerreta and Logan arrived, Smith was standing at a large worktable in the middle of the room, busily making sandwiches, then folding them in wrappers and putting them in a tray. He finished one tray, set it in one of the refrigerators, then came back to the worktable to continue the process.

"You'd be amazed at how many sandwiches I sell every day," he offered.

"Maybe not all that surprised," Cerreta replied. "They do look good."

"Here, have one." Smith handed a freshly-made sandwich to Cerreta.

"No, thank you."

"Go ahead, try it, on the house," Smith insisted, shoving the submarine sandwich at him.

"Thanks," Cerreta said. He broke the sandwich in half and handed part of it to Logan, then took a bite. "Mr. Smith, you filed a complaint with the FBI about Bart Eberwine. Do you remember that?"

"Yeah, of course I remember," Smith answered.

"I wonder if you would, sir, tell me the nature of the complaint?"

"It's pretty involved," Smith said.

"That's all right. I'll take the time to listen."

"Have you ever heard anything about hostile takeovers?"

"Yeah, sure. That's where somebody buys out a company, even if the company doesn't want to be bought out, isn't it?"

"That's it," Smith said.

"Does this have something to do with a hostile takeover?"

"That it does. Someone is trying to take over JTJ Enterprises. Bart Eberwine was signed on as a white knight, but the white knight has turned black."

"Now you've lost me."

"You'll catch up as I explain it to you," Smith promised. "First, let me tell you a little about the company that's being taken over. It's what they call a green company. Green companies, in case you didn't realize it, are the hottest things going right now."

"What are green companies?" Logan asked. "Uhmm, this sandwich is good."

"Thanks," Smith said. "Green companies are companies that deal with the environment. You know, new ways to handle waste management . . . environmentally safe methods of energy production, that sort of thing?"

"Yeah, I guess I have read a little about them," Logan replied. "Aren't they one of those companies that go into small to medium-sized cities and build incinerators that will burn solid waste and convert it to energy?"

"That's it," Smith said. "JTJ Enterprises is just such a company. And to give you an example of how hot they are, they closed last night at fifty-four dollars a share. Three months ago they were at two and a quarter."

Cerreta whistled. "From two and a quarter to fifty-four dollars in three months? I'm not much for following the market, but even I know that's quite a jump."

"Yes, it is. In fact, that's too big a jump to be explained by the company's performance. That's the kind of jump that happens when someone starts a bid for a hostile takeover. That someone is called a black knight."

"I'm curious. Why do they call them black knights?"

"In medieval mythology, black knights are always the bad guys," Smith explained. "And, as you may gather from the term, 'hostile,' black knights are the bad guys in the business world. If not bad, they are certainly unfriendly, at least as far as the target of their bid is concerned. Also, the identity of the real person behind hostile takeovers is generally unknown. Hence, the image of a black knight, hiding behind his helmet and face mask."

"Are you saying that Eberwine figures into this?"

"Yes, from both ends," Smith said. "You see, Barry, Patmore and Daigh have worked with JTJ Enterprises for several years. It was their analysis of the market that alerted JTJ to the fact that they were a target. Peter James, the CEO of JTJ, came to Barry, Patmore and Daigh to ask for help. He wanted a white knight."

"A white knight," Cerreta said. "All right, that is obviously the opposite of a black knight, but how, exactly?"

"A white knight is someone who bids against the black knight . . . it's like starting a backfire in a forest fire. The idea is to either buy so much stock that the black knight cannot get control . . . or run the price of the stock up so high that the black knight will lose interest."

"Okay, I guess I can follow that."

"Bart Eberwine was given the job of playing white knight," Smith said. "And, since he was a white knight, he was made privy to confidential information that the black knight didn't have."

"I know you said that the identity of the black knight isn't always known," Cerreta said. "But do you know who this black knight is?"

Smith chuckled. "I was wondering when you would get around to asking that question. In the hostile takeover bid for JTJ Enterprises, the black knight is a man named Costaconti."

"You don't mean Angelo Costaconti? The Mafia boss?" Logan said.

Smith nodded. "That's the man."

"You said Eberwine was mixed up in this from both sides. What do you mean?"

"Eberwine set up a corporation of his own, a company called Alchemist Projects. Alchemist Projects bought three hundred thousand shares of JTJ stock, on margin, before the market value shot up. Then, acting as the white knight—which meant he didn't have to use any of his own money, but used JTJ's own money—he bought several thousand more shares. The market couldn't stand the pressure and the price of the stock began rocketing. That made the value of his own stock shoot up . . . and remember, he bought that stock on margin in the first place, so that his actual cash outlay was minimal."

"Pretty smart," Logan said.

"Wait," Smith said. "It isn't over. Eberwine knew he had a good thing going, so in order to keep the black knight in the ball game, he sold Costaconti confidential information. The result was that Costaconti was also buying heavily. Then, when the stock reached twenty-five dollars a share, Eberwine unloaded his three hundred thousand shares."

"He must have made a killing."

"He cleared a little over five million dollars," Smith said. "He immediately came back in with two hundred thousand shares at twenty-five. As of closing last night, he was another five million ahead."

"Damn! That's ten million dollars!" Logan said. "Does anyone know this? I mean, any of the officials of the company?"

"No. This isn't the kind of thing you do in the light of day."

"Then that raises the obvious question, Mr. Smith," Cerreta said. "How do you know all this?"

Smith held up one of the sandwiches. "You see this? It makes me invisible. When I come around selling doughnuts, coffee, and sandwiches, people don't even know I'm there. Their mouths start to salivate by some involuntary reflex, their stomachs growl, their hands, reacting to this same involuntary reflex, reach down into their pockets for money then stretch out for the food, all by involuntary reflex. Their brains don't disengage from what they're thinking about, and their tongues don't stop wagging. I hear a lot of things . . . I retain some of them."

"I can see how that might be," Logan said. "But how is it that you know enough to even understand what you happen to overhear? I mean, this is pretty technical stuff, isn't it?"

Smith laughed. "You think it's all too much for a sandwich vendor, do you?"

"Yes, as a matter of fact, I do," Logan replied. "I don't mean this as a slur against your intelligence or anything, but how *do* you know the value of what you hear, when you hear it?"

"I've worked here in this very building for over fifteen years. You can't be around something that long without picking up a little. Every time I heard something I didn't understand, I would make a point to look it up. When I overheard a few of Eberwine's telephone conversations, picked up a few pieces of discarded paper, watched his buying and selling patterns, I was able to figure out exactly what he was doing."

"Are you the only one who knows this?" Cerreta asked.

"I am now. Before he was killed, Kinder knew what was going on."

"Wait a minute! Kinder knew?"

"Yes."

"How do you know he knew?"

"George Kinder was killed on Wednesday, June eleventh," Smith said. "On Tuesday night, the tenth, I overheard Eberwine and Kinder having a discussion."

"An argument?"

Smith shook his head. "No, not an argument. A discussion."

"What did you hear?"

"Kinder said, 'When you bail out of here, that golden parachute had better be big enough for both of us.' And he came down hard on the word 'better.' "

"What do you think Kinder meant by that?"

"I don't think, I know. He was threatening to expose Eberwine if Eberwine didn't pay off."

"And how did Eberwine react to the threat?"

"He said he would take care of things."

"Do you think that by 'taking care of things' Eberwine meant to pay Kinder off?"

"Eberwine put the deal together," Smith said. "I've known him for six years. I don't believe he is the kind of person who would give away half the profits of his enterprise. No, sir, I don't think he had any intention of paying off. As a matter of fact, if I didn't know how Kinder died, I would have been very suspicious."

"Mr. Smith, would you testify, in court, to everything you have told us here?"

"Yes, of course," Smith said. "But my testimony alone won't do it. You're going to have to subpoena records and sales slips to document all of his activity. It isn't going to be an easy trail to follow."

"We'll take care of that," Cerreta said. "You just be ready to testify."

"Murder?" Wentworth said. "We have him charged with second degree manslaughter and reckless endangerment, but now you want to go back and reindict Eberwine for murder?"

"Murder Two, two counts," Stone said. "Adam, this wasn't merely some confrontation that went tragically awry. This was a cold, calculated homicide. Eberwine wanted Kinder dead, so he set Teroy Brown up to do the job for him."

"Murder Two is going to be an awfully hard sell," Wentworth warned.

"We can do it, Adam. We have opportunity, hell, we've got pictures. We've got means—the means is Teroy Brown. And now we have motive. We know that Eberwine was heavily involved in fraudulent trading practices."

Wentworth picked up the report filed by Cerreta and Logan. "I don't want to get into that," he said. "That's federal."

"We don't have to get into it any deeper than to show that Eberwine was enriching himself by illegal means, and Kinder wanted to cut himself a piece of the pie. Kinder was blackmailing Eberwine, so Eberwine got rid of Kinder. It's as simple as that."

Wentworth chuckled. "That may very well be a basic truth, Counselor. But it is definitely not simple. All right, prepare your brief, we'll go back for Murder Two, but you had better dig in hard. Tom Henry is going to have a field day with this one."

"Let him have at it," Stone said. "This time I'll kick his ass."

Wentworth looked up suddenly. "That's right, you've known Henry a long time, haven't you?"

Stone nodded.

"Ben, you aren't turning this into some sort of personal duel between the two of you, are you? I seem to recall you took some heat after the von Brandenberg case.''

''I won't deny that I'm looking forward to tangling with him again,'' Stone replied. ''But, Adam, I'd push this one just as hard if Eberwine had drawn the most junior P.D. in the city for his defense. He committed murder and he damn near slipped it by us.''

''All right,'' Wentworth said. ''Go for it, and let me know if you need anything.''

The line monitor showed two men sitting on a darkened stage. A camera and camera operator, both in silhouette, were in the foreground. The chyron read: LENNIE COLE, LIVE ACCESS.

''And now, from the ACN studios in New York, it's Lennie Cole, *Live Access,*'' a well-modulated voice-over said. ''Lennie's guest tonight is Tom Henry. And now, here's Lennie Cole.''

The camera moved in for a one-shot of Lennie Cole. Lennie wore a button-up shirt with his sleeves rolled up, his collar open, and his necktie askew. A well-worn hat sat back on his head, with a tag sticking from the hat band, which read, PRESS.

''Good evening. My guest tonight is Tom Henry, one of America's most celebrated criminal lawyers. Millions watched, entranced, a few years ago, as Tom Henry conducted the brilliant defense that cleared Karl von Brandenberg of the charge of murder. Another half a million readers bought his book, which told the exciting behind-the-scenes story of that high-visibility trial. Now Tom Henry is involved in another very high-profile case. I'm talking about the murder trial of Wall Street broker, Bart Eberwine. You remember this case, folks. This is the case where two young men, both stockbrokers, were attacked in the parking lot of the athletic club where they had gone to play a game of handball. Mr. Eberwine, because he frequently carried large sums of money, was licensed to carry a gun. By coincidence, he had transported a large sum of money that very day, so he had the gun in his athletic bag as he and his friend, George Kinder, were walking to the car. They were accosted by two individuals, a scuffle ensued, and, in the scuffle, Mr. Eberwine's friend of long standing, George Kinder, was killed, stabbed by one of the attackers. Mr. Eberwine then shot one of the attackers." Lennie Cole turned toward Tom Henry. "But the attacker Eberwine shot is not the one who killed George Kinder, is it?"

"No," Tom Henry said.

"In his initial statement to the police, Eberwine claimed to have shot the man who stabbed his friend, did he not?"

"Yes, he did. But there is a simple explanation for that. When there is confusion during war, the military calls it **'the fog of war.'** Mistakes happen all the time as a result of 'the fog of war.' Sometimes with tragic consequences, such as when American troops kill American troops. Thank God the man Mr. Eberwine killed was one of the attackers, even though, in the 'fog of war,' it was not the one he thought.''

"That sounds plausible," Cole said.

Tom Henry smiled. "Let's hope that the jury shares your ability to see the logic, and realizes it is the truth."

Lennie Cole turned to stare, sincerely, into the camera. "We'll be back after this commercial."

During the commercial break, Robinette, who was eating a piece of pizza, called Ben Stone. Stone picked it up on the third ring.

"You watching ACN?" Robinette asked.

"Are you kidding? The Mets are on ESPN."

"Listen to the game on the radio," Robinette said. "You need to watch this."

"We're back with our guest, famed defense attorney Tom Henry. Mr. Henry, if I didn't say so before, it is a privilege to have you on the show," Lennie Cole said.

"And I'm very glad to be here," Henry replied.

The studio lights were flattering, Robinette thought. Henry looked more like an actor, a handsome leading actor playing the role, than an actual practicing lawyer.

"I must say that I was a little surprised that you accepted our invitation to be a guest on the show," Cole began. "In the past, you have steadfastly refused to discuss any ongoing cases."

"Yes," Henry said, brushing a cowlick back. "Well, in the past, we have tried our cases in a court of law, before a jury of the defendant's peers. More recently the trend has been to try the cases before the court of public opinion."

"In what way, sir?"

"Come on, Lennie, you know in what way. You're part of the problem." Henry smiled engagingly. "Well, not you, personally," he said. "But the profession to which you belong."

"And you feel this case is being tried before the public?"

"Yes, of course it is," Henry replied. "The videotape has been shown dozens and dozens of times. Talk shows have discussed it with advocates for both sides of the case. And, to add fuel to the fire, information is now being released as to how much money my client made through stock negotiations."

"I'm glad you brought that up, Mr. Henry. In fact, Mr. Eberwine's trading activities are currently under federal investigation for possible unlawful stock practices, are they not?"

"There is a federal investigation under way, yes," Henry said. "But as of today, Mr. Eberwine has not been indicted. Despite that, some members of your profession, the same people who, just a few days ago were making a hero of him, would now have him charged, tried, and convicted. The truth, of course, lies in that great area to which all news media people are totally blind—somewhere in between. He is neither the hero they once thought, nor the villain they are now trying to make of him. Anyway, whether his stock dealings are illegal, or unethical, or just plain annoying to people who are jealous of his success, they have nothing at all to do with the case at hand; to wit, did Bart Eberwine murder George Kinder and Clarence Ellis? And the answer to that is a resounding no!"

"Let's take a look at the videotape, shall we?" Cole suggested. "I'm sure there is practically no one in America who hasn't seen this tape, but I'd like to have your comments as we watch it. And by the way, before we show it, we need to thank WACN in New York for allowing us to use it."

As the scene played out on the TV screen, Robinette watched it for what had to be the fiftieth time. He knew it frame by frame, and yet he watched it as closely this time as he did the first time it was shown to him.

"Mr. Eberwine and Mr. Kinder are not yet in the picture," Tom Henry explained, "but you can see, here, that Ellis and Brown are already in a confrontational mode. I wish we had sound, but we don't need sound to read the body language. If you will notice, both Brown and Ellis have their shoulders hunched forward, their knees slightly bent, their arms hanging loose. These are two powerfully built men, both with a long history of violent assault. What you are looking at right now, Lennie, is as terrifying as if you were looking right down the barrel of a loaded .45.

"And now here come Mr. Kinder and Mr. Eberwine. As you can see, Mr. Eberwine is replying to the challenge and abusive language issued by Ellis and Brown."

"Yes, but according to some of the articles I have read, this was all expected, wasn't it?" Cole asked. "By that I mean, hasn't Eberwine admitted that he arranged to have these two men there to set up a confrontation?"

"Yes, that's true," Henry said. "But if you will read Eberwine's body language, you will notice that he appears to be somewhat confused and a little frightened at this point. He realizes, here, that this is obviously not what he planned. And look, here. Do you see how he's making a motion for Kinder to step out of the way? He's being protective of his friend, which is what he had in mind all along. That is hardly the action of someone who would purposely pick a fight in order to expose his friend to the possibility of being stabbed.

"And here's one more critical point, Lennie. Do you see, here, where Mr. Ellis is, apparently, reaching for a knife? Now, the prosecution has made a great deal over the fact that my client shot Ellis instead of Brown, who actually did the stabbing.

"And here it comes. Look quickly, for it's over in an instant. There Kinder steps forward, there is a slashing movement from Brown's arm, though I would like to point out to our viewers that as Kinder is now standing between Mr. Eberwine and Teroy Brown, it is impossible for him to see that. He sees only that his friend is going down with a stab wound in his chest, and he fires at the person whom he now thinks represents the most danger to himself. And that would be Clarence Ellis, who is bigger, closer, and, as I pointed out earlier, had already made a motion as if going for a knife."

"Yes, but there was no other knife," Lennie said. "The police searched the area thoroughly, and no knife was found."

"You cannot prove a negative," Henry replied. "The fact that no knife was found does not mean no knife existed. But in truth, whether or not a second knife existed is totally irrelevant. If Mr. Eberwine was convinced that Clarence Ellis was going for a knife, he was totally justified in firing in what he believed to be the defense of his life, and the life of his friend.''

"I must say, that is a fascinating look at the tape from a perspective we haven't seen before,'' Cole said. He looked toward the camera. "We'll be back with your calls, after this.''

Robinette returned to the phone.

"You're watching?'' he asked.

"Yeah,'' Stone's voice growled.

"Why is he giving away his defense?''

Stone chuckled. "Come on, Paul, you've played baseball. You've showed bunt, then swung for the bleachers, haven't you?''

Robinette laughed. "I've swung for them,'' he replied. "I didn't hit them all that often.''

"If he's showing that, he has more . . . much more.''

"Damn,'' Robinette said. "What he's showing us is pretty good.''

"They're back,'' Stone said.

"All right, we'll take your calls now,'' Cole said. "Hello, Hillsboro, Illinois, you're on the air.''

"Yes,'' a female caller said. "Mr. Henry, if you think there's too much publicity about this trial, why are you on the Lennie Cole show?''

"Good question,'' Cole said, switching the

caller off and fixing Tom Henry with his patented look of sincerity. "Mr. Henry, why are you here?"

"Lennie, I can't let my case be constantly attacked in public and make no effort whatever to defend it," Henry replied. "No matter how weak the prosecution's case is, if they keep chip, chip, chipping away, they're going to wear down logic and common sense to the degree that some people might actually begin to believe them. If public opinion turns against my client, then the jury will carry that weight with them into the deliberation room. I have to neutralize the negative press."

"Understandable," Cole said. "Montgomery, Alabama, you're on."

"Isn't what you've got here a matter of racial intolerance?" a male voice asked. "I mean, let's face it. If Eberwine and Kinder had seen two white men standing by their car, none of this would've happened, would it?"

"No, I don't think race has anything to do with it," Henry replied. "Ellis and Cole were clearly threatening individuals. If two white men—or two Orientals, for that matter—had approached George Kinder and Bart Eberwine in the same belligerent manner, it would have been just as frightening, and given those circumstances, the results may well have been the same."

"Don't go away," Cole said, looking at the camera again. "We'll be back for more of your calls, after this."

Stone had seen enough, and he picked up the remote to switch back to ESPN. It was the bottom of the third and the Cardinals were up.

"That home run came with two men on, and the Redbirds now lead five to one," the announcer said.

"Shit," Stone said disgustedly.

Chapter Six

Judge Harlan T. Jones of New York Superior Court had tufts of white hair above each ear and a snow-white moustache so full and bushy that it nearly hid his mouth. The white hair seemed even more brilliant when contrasted with his dark skin; someone once made the remark that he looked a little like Uncle Ben on the boxes of Uncle Ben's Converted Rice. It was not a comparison the African American judge appreciated, and no one who wanted to stay in his favor ever made it again. And, since Judge Jones was, because of his position, a very powerful man, everyone wanted to stay in his favor.

Ben Stone had never tried a case before

Judge Jones, so he had no personal feelings one way or the other as to how to react to the draw. Judge Jones was known to be a stickler for minute adherence to procedure. On the one hand, this meant that every i had to be dotted and every t crossed if they were to be certain that Eberwine wouldn't walk on some technicality. On the other hand, it might also limit Tom Henry's flamboyant defense style. Evidently, Henry thought that as well, for Stone learned, just before the jury selection began, that Henry had tried, unsuccessfully, to have the judge changed.

On balance, then, Stone believed that he was probably better off with Judge Jones than without him, if for no other reason than that Tom Henry had wanted him changed.

Equally as important as the judge was the selection of the jury, and here at least the counselors did not have to depend entirely on the luck of the draw. The prospective jurors could be questioned and challenged. Counselors for prosecution and defense could reject a juror for cause, if they could convince Judge Jones of the predisposition of that juror to prejudice toward either side. A few jurors could be rejected for no reason at all, just because there was something about them that didn't feel right. These were called preemptory challenges, and they were like bonuses, not to be squandered, but

hand. "I would like to exercise preemptory removal on this juror, Your Honor," he said, without even standing.

"Very well," Judge Jones said. "Mr. Austin, thank you for your time. Your services will not be needed for this jury. You are excused."

Austin left the courtroom with a confused expression on his face, not quite understanding by what process he had been eliminated.

"We won that one," Stone said, smiling.

"What do you mean?"

"I wanted him excused," he said. "But I didn't want to waste a preemptory challenge to do it, so I set him up for Tom Henry to get rid of him for me."

"Why did you want him out?"

"I overheard him talking to a couple of the others on the jury panel this morning," Stone said. "He was talking about an old movie he watched on cable last night . . . and how much he enjoyed it."

"A movie?"

"The movie was *Death Wish*," Stone said. "You remember the one, don't you? Where Charles Bronson plays a vigilante?"

"Yes, I remember the movie."

"What we don't want is a case of transferral where Tom Henry takes Mr. Austin's admiration of a fictional movie character and manages to convince him that Bart Eberwine was merely filling that role."

"Right. Good move," Robinette said, chuckling.

As it turned out, though, two could play the same game, for sometime later, Stone found himself in the same situation. A juror had responded to Henry's questions in such a way as to make him seem likely to vote for acquittal, even before the trial began. Stone excluded him, then caught, out of the corner of his eye, a satisfied smile on Henry's face.

"Damn," he said to Robinette under his breath. "It looks like Tom got me on that one."

After the exchange of preemptories, it was obvious that neither counselor would be able to manipulate the other. As a result, they abandoned the risky business of trying to trick each other, and settled down to selecting or discarding the jurors according to what was best for their own case. By evening the jury had been selected. It consisted of three white men and four white women, one Hispanic man, two black men and one black woman. There were five military veterans, three of whom had been in combat. Two of the jurors were school teachers, one was a bank clerk, two were housewives, one owned a restaurant, one was a mechanic for an airline, two were accountants, two were sales clerks, and one was retired from the merchant marine.

When the jury was sworn and seated, Judge Jones looked toward the counselors' tables.

"Is the defense ready?"

"Defense is ready, Your Honor," Tom Henry replied, half rising from his chair in deference.

"Prosecution?"

"Prosecution is ready, Your Honor," Stone answered.

"Very well, we will proceed. Prosecution may present its case," he said.

Stone nodded at Robinette, who stood up, subconsciously checked that his jacket was buttoned, then began to address the court.

"Your Honor, ladies and gentlemen of the jury, we of the prosecution, representing the people of New York, are going to prove that Bart Eberwine is guilty of premeditated murder. His scheme was particularly diabolical in that he played upon the fear that grips every innocent citizen in this or any other city in America—the fear of being set upon by armed and dangerous men.

"According to Eberwine's initial story, he and George Kinder were going to their car when they were attacked, apparently at random. Eberwine then, according to his initial story, defended them by using his pistol to kill one of the attackers.

"That was his story, but in fact the first part of the fabrication began to fall apart very early, when Eberwine *admitted* that the attack wasn't random at all. Eberwine *admitted* that he had arranged for the attack to take place, supposedly to engender some sense of gratitude in his friend and thus gain some business advantage.

"You have to admit that even if it were true, that would be a bizarre plan." Robinette looked down and shook his head. "But the truth, ladies and gentlemen, is much more bizarre, even to the point of being macabre. The truth is, Bart Eberwine set this entire scenario in motion with the sole intention of inciting Teroy Brown and Clarence Ellis into doing just what they did. He *wanted* Brown and Ellis to lash out, and they did. As a result, Eberwine's plan worked perfectly. Kinder was killed, just as Eberwine intended.

"On the surface that would appear to be a very risky way to commit murder. After all, wasn't Eberwine putting himself in danger as well?

"The answer, of course, is that it *was* a risky way to commit murder, and Eberwine was counting on that perception to isolate him from suspicion. However, Eberwine did have a circuit breaker in place. You see, Bart Eberwine was carrying a pistol, and there is an old adage among street fighters. In a fight between a person with a knife and a person with a gun, the person with the knife will always lose. Eberwine was the one with the gun. He didn't figure to lose.

"The task before the prosecution will be to prove the contention I have just advanced. It will be a difficult task, but that is by design. Bart Eberwine is a highly intelligent and very clever man, and he intended the prosecution's task to be difficult. In fact, he intended our task to be impossible.

"And finally the question that must be asked is, Why would Eberwine want George Kinder killed? What is the motive? This is the easy part, ladies and gentlemen. The *way* Eberwine killed Kinder is complex and difficult to sort out, but the *why* is as old as mankind. The motive is greed. We will prove that Bart Eberwine was engaged in fraudulent stock manipulation which enriched him to the tune of millions of dollars. George Kinder discovered the scheme and wanted to be a part of it . . . suggesting that his silence could only be ensured if he *were* a part of it.

"The challenge that has been thrown down before the people is worthy of our most exacting efforts. The challenge that we will lay before you is worthy of your most exacting analysis. But in the end, you will see, you will believe, and you will find the verdict of guilty."

When Robinette sat down, Stone reached over and squeezed his wrist by way of congratulations for a good opening statement.

Judge Jones appeared to be studying something for a moment, then cleared his throat and looked toward Tom Henry.

"Does counsel for the defense wish to make an opening statement at this time?" he asked.

"I do, Your Honor," Tom Henry replied. He sat in his chair for a long moment before he stood up and turned toward the jury.

"Ladies and gentlemen of the jury, we *do* have the facts on our side. In fact, if the defense were mute, we could still make this case, for we have a video which will show, in graphic detail, exactly what happened.

"The facts are these. Bart Eberwine did arrange for a staged confrontation. Such things are done all the time . . . this is what is called 'street theater,' ladies and gentlemen. It has been used successfully for years by civil rights activists, antiwar protestors, prochoice and prolife proponents, and, more recently, by groups who are active in AIDS programs. In Mr. Eberwine's case, the street theater was business-related. Unfortunately, this particular piece of street theater turned tragic. One of the participants of the street theater went berserk and, much to Mr. Eberwine's surprise, attacked them with a knife. Bart Eberwine had no choice then but to defend himself. He killed one of the attackers, but not before one of the attackers killed George Kinder.

"These are facts, ladies and gentlemen, and they will be substantiated not only by Mr. Eberwine's own testimony, but by your own eyes when you view the videotape.

"With their oratory, the prosecution is going to try and convince you that you do not see what you think you see. They would have you believe that black is white and up is down. They are going to try and get you to disregard the facts of the case, and find a verdict of guilty, *beyond all reasonable doubt*. A few moments ago Mr. Robinette admitted that the task before the prosecution would be difficult. I suggest to you that Mr. Robinette is a master of understatement. Difficult? It isn't going to be difficult, ladies and gentlemen. It is going to be impossible! The facts will speak for themselves . . . and you will return a verdict of not guilty."

Ben Stone drummed his fingers on the table as he watched Tom Henry return to the defendant's table. The son of a bitch was good, there was no getting around that. Stone felt a surge of adrenaline as he anticipated the battle before them. Damn, he was actually looking forward to this. He smiled.

"What is it?" Robinette whispered.

"What?"

"You were smiling."

"Sorry. Just a random thought," Stone replied without elaboration.

Judge Jones cleared his throat. "Prosecution may call the first witness," he said.

Stone then stood up.

"Your Honor, the state calls Teroy Brown to the stand."

Teroy Brown was dressed in dark trousers, a white shirt, and a light gray jacket. His hair was neatly cut and he had a fresh shave. He was sworn in, then took his seat on the witness stand.

"Mr. Brown," Stone began. "Did you kill George Kinder?"

"Yes," Brown answered. "I killed him."

"How did you kill him, Mr. Brown?"

"I stabbed him."

Stone walked over to the exhibit table and picked up a switchblade knife. The knife was tagged with a large exhibit tag. He turned toward Brown and held the knife out before him.

"Is this the knife you used?"

"Yeah, that's the one," Brown said. Then he corrected himself. "I mean, yes sir, that is the knife I used."

"Why did you kill George Kinder, Mr. Brown?"

"I don't know."

"You don't know? You killed someone and you don't know why?"

"Yeah, well, I don't know why none of it happened like it did," Brown said. "All we was supposed to do was just scare 'em. You know, just put the mouth on 'em. Nobody was s'posed to even get hurt, let alone get killed."

"What do you mean, that was what you were *supposed* to do?"

"I mean it was my job," Brown said, as casually as if he were describing a day at the office. "You see, me an' Clarence worked for Fast Eddie, and he's the one sent us down there."

"That would be Edward Turner?"

"Yeah, Edward Turner," Brown said. "Only, nobody calls him that. Ever'body calls him Fast Eddie."

"What kind of work did you do for Fast Eddie?"

"Me an' Clarence, we was adjusters," Brown replied.

"Adjusters? Were you also sometimes called 'slack men'?"

"Slack men, yeah. You could call us that."

"Mr. Brown, would you tell the court what an 'adjuster,' or 'slack man,' does?"

"Whenever somebody would stiff Fast Eddie or one of his girls, Fast Eddie would have me an' Clarence to take care of 'em."

"What do you mean by take care of them?"

"You know. We'd talk to 'em, threaten to go upside their head if they didn't straighten out."

"Did you actually have to 'go upside their heads' very often?"

"Not very often," Brown answered. "Most of the time all we had to do was just badmouth 'em. We'd get 'em so scared that if they owed any money, they'd come across soon enough."

"Have you ever killed anyone before?"

"No, never," Brown insisted. "This was the first time anything like that ever happened."

"Why did it happen this time, Mr. Brown?"

"I don't really know why it happened," Brown replied. "I mean, like I told you, it wasn't s'posed to happen at all. And the thing is, when it *did* happen, I wound up cuttin' the wrong man." Brown pointed to Bart Eberwine. "That's the one I wanted to cut."

"I thought you said no one was supposed to get hurt. Why did you want to cut Eberwine?"

"'Cause he started goin' off on me, man. I mean, I ain't goin' stand by an' let nobody go off on me the way he done."

"By, 'going off on you,' you mean what?"

"Goin' off, man," Brown said again. "You know, like, callin' me a nigger an' tellin' me he was goin' whip my black ass. That sort of thing. The dude was crazy, man. It was like he was just askin' me to cut 'im up."

"Objection, Your Honor," Henry said.

"Sustained."

"Mr. Brown, would you tell us in your own words just what happened?" Stone asked.

"Yeah. Well, Fast Eddie sent me and Clarence down to this club an' tol' us to wait out in the parkin' lot by a silver BMW. He give us the license number so we'd know which car. He told us there'd be two dudes comin' out of the club, and when they come to the car, we was s'posed to start in on 'em."

"You planned to just harass them verbally?"

"Yeah, that's all, I swear," Brown said. "But like I said, the moment the two dudes come out of the club, the one mother—" Brown halted in mid-word, then coughed in embarrassment. "I mean the one dude, he started yellin' at us, sayin' things like 'What you two niggers doin' there?' and, 'Get your black asses away from that car,' and things like that."

"Did he have a gun in his hand?"

"I didn't see no gun, no."

"All right. Then what did you do in reaction to his challenging language?"

"Well, right off I could see this wasn't goin' like it was s'posed to. We was s'posed to be tellin' him what we was goin' to do. Instead, he was doin' all the badmouthin'. Real fast, I got pissed, and I told 'im if he wanted some of this black ass, he'd better come get it."

"And did he?"

"Yeah, he come toward us, still shoutin' at us."

"Was Kinder with him?"

"Yes and no," Brown replied. "That is, Kinder was with him, but he wasn't doin' none of the yellin' and shoutin'. Fact is, Kinder was one scared dude, man. He kept beggin' Eberwine to shut up."

"Then why is it, Mr. Brown, that Kinder was the one you stabbed?"

"Like I said, I didn't mean to cut him," Brown explained. "I mean, one moment I had my knife out, headin' toward the loudmouthed dude, thinkin' I'm goin' cut him up good, and the next moment Kinder is in my face, wavin' money at me. I shoved him back—I swear, that's all I meant to do, just shove him back—and the next thing you know, he's goin' down, bleedin' like a stuck pig. I don't even remember stabbin' him, but I know I did."

"What happened after that?"

"I was standin' there lookin' at this dude I stabbed, when I heard a couple of gunshots. They come real close together, 'bang-bang,' like that. I looked up and saw that the other white dude, Eberwine, had just taken down Clarence."

"Were you surprised that he shot Clarence instead of you?"

"I was surprised as hell, man. And scared I was goin' to be next."

"What did you do then?"

"I hauled ass," Brown answered, and those in the gallery tittered in amusement. It was not necessary for Judge Jones to use his gavel or to say anything. His stare was enough to quiet them.

"Mr. Brown, after you were arrested, you were put in a lineup, were you not?"

"Yeah," Brown replied.

"And two eyewitnesses identified you as being one of the men involved in the incident, and the one who ran. Is that right?"

"Yeah."

"The two eyewitnesses claim to have seen you there. Were they speaking the truth? Were you there?"

"Yeah, I just told you."

"Bart Eberwine viewed the same lineup. Tell me, Mr. Brown, do you believe Eberwine saw you clearly enough to identify you?"

"Objection, Your Honor. Whether this witness believes Eberwine saw him clearly enough to identify him calls for the conclusion and judgment of another person's knowledge."

"Sustained."

"Mr. Brown, did Bart Eberwine identify you?"

"No."

"Why do you suppose he did not identify you?"

"Objection, Your Honor! Calls for a conclusion!"

"Your Honor," Stone said, "if two people who are separated by only a few feet are involved in a confrontation of this nature, it seems only natural that they would be able to recognize each other upon seeing each other a second time. Since Mr. Eberwine claimed not to recognize Mr. Brown, a natural question would be, why not?"

Judge Jones stroked his chin as he thought for a moment. Then he said, "No, Mr. Stone. The objection is sustained."

"Very well, Your Honor," Stone said. He turned back toward the witness. "Mr. Brown, did Eberwine get a good look at you?"

"Objection, Your Honor!"

"Sustained," Judge Jones said. He looked at Stone. "Mr. Stone, disabuse yourself of any idea that you might score with the jury in some way by repeatedly calling for a conclusion from this witness," he scolded. "I simply will not allow it."

"Yes, Your Honor," Stone replied, duly chastised. He started toward the table, then stopped and turned toward the witness again. "Mr. Brown, when next you saw Eberwine, did you recognize him as the person with whom you had the confrontation?"

"Objection!" Tom Henry shouted.

"Overruled," Judge Jones. "You may answer the question, Mr. Brown."

"Yeah," Brown said. "I recognized him."

"Thank you. No further questions, Your Honor."

"Mr. Henry?" Judge Jones said.

"Mr. Brown, do you know a James Evans?" Henry asked.

"What about him?"

"Just answer the question, Mr. Brown. Do you know James Evans?"

"Yeah," Brown said, looking at the floor. "I know him."

"In what way do you know him?"

"I, uh, loaned him some money once."

"Did he repay you?"

"Yeah, he paid me back."

"Did he repay you promptly, or did you have to persuade him . . . 'badmouth' I believe you called it?"

"It took a little persuasion," Brown admitted with a crooked grin.

"And did that persuasion result in Mr. Evans being hospitalized for injuries from the beating you gave him?"

"Objection, Your Honor. We are not trying Mr. Brown for assault against James Evans."

"Your Honor, I merely wish to establish Teroy Brown's background of violence," Henry replied. "The prosecution would have us believe that Teroy Brown only spoke harshly to his victims. And yet here is a clear example to the contrary."

"Overruled," Judge Jones said. "You may continue."

"Thank you, Your Honor. Mr. Brown, you testified that you were instructed to meet Bart Eberwine and George Kinder at the parking lot of the Executive Stress Athletic Club. Were you told to harm them in any way?"

"No, I already told you, all I was s'posed to do was put the mouth on 'em."

"I see. So, when you took it upon yourself to attack them, you were, in fact, violating the instructions you had been given. Is that right?"

"I don't know what you mean."

"Were you told to kill George Kinder?"

"No."

"But you did kill him. You have admitted that."

"Yeah, I killed him."

"Because you lost your temper?"

"Who wouldn't lose their temper the way—"

"Just answer the question, Mr. Brown. You didn't go to the parking lot to kill anyone, did you?"

"No."

"But once you were there, you lost your temper and you did kill someone. Is that correct?"

"Yeah, but like I said—"

"No further questions, Your Honor," Henry said, interrupting Teroy Brown's response.

"Redirect?" Judge Jones asked Stone.

"Mr. Brown," Stone asked, walking over to the witness. "You said the defendant was 'badmouthing' you, did you not?"

"Yeah, like I said, he was callin' me nigger and sayin'—"

Stone waved his hand to interrupt Brown's response. "At the moment the specifics are not important," he said. "What is important is *when* the defendant started 'badmouthing' you."

"Hell, he started in soon as he saw us," Brown replied. "I mean, from the moment he come out the door."

"And was this before you started 'badmouthing' him? Or was this in response to something you had already said?"

"I ain't said nothin' yet," Brown replied. "And next thing you know, he had me so pissed off I wasn't in no mood to say nothin'. All I was wantin' then was to go upside his head."

"Thank you. No further questions."

"Gentlemen, the seating of the jury, the opening statements, and the cross-examination of the first witness have consumed most of the day," Judge Jones said. "Therefore I am going to call a recess until tomorrow morning at nine o'clock."

Chapter
Seven

"**C**erreta," Cerreta said into the phone the next morning.

"Sergeant Cerreta, this is Special Agent Bixler of the FBI."

"Yeah, Bixler, what can I do for you?" Cerreta asked.

"A mutual friend of ours, Sally Bateman, told me you're the one working the investigation on the Eberwine case," Bixler said.

"That's right."

"We need to talk."

"What about? You have some information for me?"

"As a matter of fact, I do," Bixler said. "Unfortunately, you can't use it."

"What do you mean, I can't use it?"

"Look, I don't want to talk about this over the phone. Can we meet for coffee somewhere?"

"I'm bringing my partner."

"That would be Mike Logan? Yeah, sure, that'll be okay," Bixler said. "Listen, you know Danny's place on Lexington? Between Forty-eighth and Forty-ninth?"

"I know the place."

"Half an hour," Bixler said.

Cerreta hung up the phone, then nodded at Logan, who had been following one side of the conversation from his desk.

"Let's go see the captain," Cerreta suggested.

"That's all he said? That he had some information for you, but you can't use it?" Captain Cragen asked.

"That's it," Cerreta said.

"Well, I guess you'd better go see what he has to say."

"Captain, that might not be a good idea," Logan suggested.

"What do you mean? You don't think you should even talk to him?"

"Mike and I were talking, Captain, and he has a point," Cerreta said. "Maybe we shouldn't go see this guy."

"Why not?"

"Suppose he tells us something we already know," Logan said. "And suppose he has some sort of federal judge's injunction against using that information. We'd wind up shooting ourselves in the foot."

"Yeah, I see what you mean," Captain Cragen said. He leaned back in his chair and stroked his chin for a moment. He looked over at Logan. "Mike, how far do you trust Sally?"

"She's always been straight with me."

"Call her, see if she knows this guy, or if he's just used her name. If she'll vouch for him, I think you should take the chance."

"All right."

"But play everything by ear," Cragen added. "Don't commit yourself to anything without letting the D.A. know what's happening."

Cerreta leaned against the front of the desk drinking coffee, while Logan talked to Sally. When the conversation was finished, Logan glanced over at him.

"She says he's worth talking to," he said. "But we may not like the price."

"What does that mean?"

"She didn't want to say over the telephone. Phil, you ask me, we have no choice. We have to meet with the guy."

Cerreta put the cup down. "All right," he said. "Let's go."

Danny's was a street-level coffee shop that proudly advertised: "Breakfast served at any hour of the day!" The customers were served at a dozen small tables, as well as a long, plastic-topped counter that ran along one wall. Behind the counter, in addition to the fry griddle, there were two large coffee urns and two zinc sinks. On the wall behind the counter was a large menu featuring the bill of fare, and a hand-painted sign touted the "Special of the Day," a bacon-lettuce-tomato and avocado sandwich, for $2.25.

A large-bellied man wearing a white apron and a white chef's cap was at the griddle, frying hamburgers. The smell of frying hamburger meat mixed with the accumulated smells of years of short-order specialties, giving the coffee shop a familiar if not unpleasant aroma.

Though Cerreta had never met Special Agent Bixler, he saw a conservatively dressed man hunching over a cup of coffee at one of the back tables and knew immediately this was his man.

"Bixler?" he asked quietly.

"Yes," the man answered. "Thanks for coming, Cerreta." Bixler looked at Logan.

"Detective Mike Logan," Logan said.

"Yeah. Have a seat."

Two cups of coffee appeared almost as soon as the men were seated.

"Look," Bixler said after the waiter withdrew. "I won't beat around the bush on this thing. I've heard you were investigating Eberwine's investments."

"Yes, we are," Cerreta said.

"Why?" Bixler asked.

"Why? Because we're investigating a murder case, that's why," Cerreta answered. "And we have to look at all aspects of it."

"But don't you already have corroborating testimony from witnesses?"

"Look, Bixler, what is it you want?" Cerreta asked.

"I don't want you looking into anything else dealing with Eberwine's finances," Bixler said.

"What? Are you crazy? Why would you ask such a thing?"

"For the last four years the mob has managed to launder millions of dollars of racketeering money. That money, acquired through drug deals and other illegal operations, is *our* money, and once it gets into the mainstream, we lose it."

"Our money?"

"The federal government," Bixler said. "You know how that works."

"Yeah, I know how it works," Cerreta said.

"What has that to do with our investigation of Eberwine?"

"We've had Eberwine's phone tapped for six months now," Bixler said. "He's become Costaconti's personal Laundromat."

"Then we're right. There is a motive," Logan said.

Bixler chuckled. "Oh, you are even more right than you know." He reached into his shirt pocket and pulled out a cassette tape. "Here's something for you. You can listen to it, but you can't use it."

"What is it?"

"It's a little something we picked up from the phone tap," Bixler said. He held up his finger. "As I said, you can listen to it. But we will not allow you to use it."

"I don't get it," Logan said. "What good does it do us to listen to it if we can't use it?"

Bixler drained the rest of his coffee, then stood up. "I'll leave that for you boys to decide," he said. "You're pretty smart guys, aren't you? Take care of this for me, will you? I had a bacon and egg sandwich."

"We can meet in here," Stone said to Cerreta and Logan as he, the two detectives, and Robinette stepped into a small room in the courthouse and closed the door. "What have you got for us?"

"We have a tape for you guys to listen to," Cerreta answered. "The first voice you hear will be Eberwine's." He punched on the tape player.

"We've got a problem," Eberwine said.

"What sort of problem?" another voice replied.

"Who is that?" Stone asked.

"The tape log says this is Paulie Sangreo. Ever heard of him?"

"Yeah, I've heard of him," Stone said. "He's one of Costaconti's enforcers."

"One of the other brokers here, a guy named Kinder, George Kinder, has figured out the game plan," Eberwine's voice continued.

"Is he making threats?"

"Not directly. He's asking to be cut in. I think that implies a threat, don't you?"

"Just a minute."

There was only side-tone noise for a moment.

"The next voice you hear will be the Man himself," Cerreta said. "Angelo Costaconti."

"What do you want?" Costaconti asked.

"Kinder wants a golden parachute."

"Sounds like you've got a problem."

"It isn't just my problem," Eberwine said. *"I would think that a problem of this magnitude would affect us all."*

"Yeah? In what way?"

"Well, if he doesn't get what he wants, he may get talkative. That could ruin everything."

"Don't let him get talkative."

"I don't have any choice. He's demanding money. A lot of money."

"Is this a shakedown?"

"A . . . a shakedown?" Eberwine asked, obviously frightened by the accusation. *"No, no, of course not. What makes you ask such a thing?"*

"Because I don't know why you're bringing this up to me," Costaconti replied. *"Are you telling me you need money to take care of things?"*

"No, nothing like that."

"Then what do you want?"

"I thought maybe you could, uh, fix it so that his parachute doesn't open, if you know what I mean."

"I know what you mean," Costaconti replied. That was followed by a long beat of silence.

"Well, I thought maybe you could take care of the problem."

"Take care of the problem?"

"Yes."

"How?"

"You know how. By doing whatever you do when problems like this come up."

"You're beatin' around the bush, my friend. What is it you want?"

"I told you, I want you to fix it so that his parachute doesn't open. I want you to make the problem go away. I want you to make him go away," Eberwine said.

Costaconti chuckled. *"Fix it so his parachute*

doesn't open . . . make him go away. You want us to do it, but you can't even say in plain English what you want us to do, can you?"

"This is a little out of my field," Eberwine said.

"Listen, you got a problem with Kinder, you take care of it. You hear what I'm sayin'? He's your problem, not ours. Only do whatever you're goin' to do pretty quick because I don't want obstacles like that in the way of our doin' business. You understand? You take care of it."

"How?"

"What do you mean, how? You're a smart man. You figure out how. The only advice I got for you is to make it permanent. And get it done before we do any more business together."

"All right," Eberwine said. "I'll get it done."

Cerreta turned the tape player off. "That's it," he said. "That's what I wanted you guys to hear."

"Jesus, that's dynamite," Stone said, reaching for it. "That'll blow Henry's case right out of the water."

"No," Cerreta said, shaking his head. "You can't use it."

"What? What do you mean we can't use it?"

"Captain Cragen has already checked with your boss, and they've checked downtown and with the feds. The restrictions against our using this tape are iron tight. We can't use it."

"Shit!" Stone said. "Shit!" He smacked his

fist into the palm of his hand and turned away from the table, then walked over to look out through a window. He stared at the traffic below for a long moment before turning back toward Cerreta and Logan.

"Do you realize we have a murderer in there?" he asked. "A murderer who may very well go free because we can't use this?"

"Come on, Ben, you think Phil likes telling us we can't have it?" Robinette asked. "He's not the one that's keeping us from using it."

"I know, I know," Stone said, waving his hand. He sighed again, then put his hand on Cerreta's shoulder and squeezed it. "I know it isn't you, Phil. It's just . . . well, it's damn frustrating knowing that we've got the weapon, right here, to wrap this case up, and we can't use it. Why did you let me hear it in the first place?"

"I don't know," Cerreta replied. He shrugged. "Maybe I thought you would be able to get something out of it."

"Yeah. A case of ulcers," Stone replied with a grunting laugh.

"Look at it this way," Robinette suggested. "At least we know that we're right. That ought to mean something, shouldn't it?"

Stone looked at Robinette for a moment, then, inexplicably, he laughed.

"Yes, my friend, it means we have the

strength of ten because our hearts are pure and our cause is just," he teased. "Come on, let's see what we can do about taking our pure hearts and just cause into the courtroom to kick a little ass."

When Fast Eddie took the oath, those who knew him best almost didn't recognize him. Gone was the flamboyant dress of the street, and in its place was an ultraconservative gray suit. After he was sworn, he took the witness stand and crossed his legs.

Robinette handled the questioning of this witness.

"Mr. Turner, what is your occupation?" he asked.

"I'm a manager," Fast Eddie said.

"A manager? What, or who, do you manage?"

"I have several clients," Fast Eddie said. "Ladies, mostly, who provide escort service for tourists and others who would like to be shown around the city."

"Mr. Turner, isn't it true that you procure girls for sexual purposes?"

"When you put men and women together for a social evening, there's not much tellin' what's goin' to happen," Fast Eddie replied. "If they want to get it on, that's their business."

"But isn't that exactly what the men who

come to see the women you . . . manage . . . expect to happen?''

Fast Eddie sighed. "Yeah," he said. "I guess you could say that.''

"Thank you for your candor, Mr. Turner," Robinette said. "Now, I ask you to look at the defendant and tell me if you have ever seen him before.''

"Yeah, I've seen him.''

"Was he a regular customer of yours?''

"No, he wasn't no customer. I actually never saw him but one time before all this happened.''

"Would you please tell the court the nature of that one meeting?''

"Well, it was like I said before," Fast Eddie said. "I was standin' near my car, mindin' my own business, when Eberwine walks up. 'My good man,' he says.'' Fast Eddie chuckled. "I ain't never been called 'my good man' before— not for real. And here was this fella callin' me 'my good man' just pretty as you please.''

"And what did he want?''

"He wanted somethin' crazy . . . real crazy," Fast Eddie replied. "He wanted me to have a couple of guys come down to the parkin' lot of some athletic club.''

"Would that be the Executive Stress Athletic Club?'' Stone asked.

"The Executive Stress—yeah, that's the

place," Fast Eddie said. "Anyway, he wanted me to send a couple of guys down there to go off on two men. And here's the funny part—he was one of them two men."

"Did he tell you why he made such an unusual request?"

"He didn't say why and I didn't ask. I figured different strokes for different folks, you know what I mean? Maybe he's one of them kind that have to be scared shitless before they can get it on with a woman."

"Objection, Your Honor."

"Sustained," Judge Jones said.

"Mr. Turner, did you accept the assignment?"

"Yeah, are you kiddin'? For five thousand dollars, I accepted it. 'Course, I was s'posed to get another five thousand, only the dude never come through."

"You sent Clarence Ellis and Teroy Brown to a planned confrontation with Bart Eberwine and George Kinder?"

"Yeah."

"And this was at the request of Bart Eberwine?"

"That's right."

"Did you tell Ellis and Brown that one of the men they were going to menace had, himself, set things up?"

"No."

"Why didn't you tell them?"

"I figured if they knew that, they might find out how much he paid, and if they knew that, they might want more than their normal cut."

"You said you were offered ten thousand dollars."

"But I was only paid five thousand."

"And how much did you pay Ellis and Brown?"

"Five hundred each, same as always."

"Thank you, Mr. Turner. Your witness, Counselor."

"Mr. Turner, were you surprised when you heard that the confrontation between Ellis and Brown had gotten violent?" Tom Henry asked.

"Yeah, very surprised."

"Why were you surprised?"

"Like I been sayin', nobody was s'posed to get hurt."

"In fact, didn't Bart Eberwine specify, even as he was setting things up, that no one was to be hurt?"

"That's what he said."

"No further questions, Your Honor."

"Redirect, Mr. Robinette?"

Robinette stood up but he didn't leave the table. "Mr. Turner, would you say that Ellis and Brown were men with volatile personalities?"

"Say what?"

"Were they quick to anger?"

Fast Eddie smiled. "Yeah, well, they wasn't somebody you'd want to mess with, you know what I mean? You do, they be goin' upside your head."

"It would be easy then for the defendant to incite them to violence?"

"Objection, Your Honor," Henry literally shouted. "That calls for conjecture."

"Your Honor, I submit that Mr. Turner enjoyed a rather unique relationship with Ellis and Brown, one that would allow him, perhaps more than anyone else, to make such a conjecture."

"Objection overruled. You may answer the question."

"What is the question?"

"Mr. Turner, knowing Ellis and Brown as you did, do you believe Bart Eberwine—or anyone, for that matter—could make them angry enough to attack?"

"That wouldn't be hard to do at all," Turner replied.

"Thank you. No further questions."

"Witness may step down. Prosecution, call your next witness."

"Your Honor, the state calls John Smith."

John Smith was called, sworn in, then seated in the witness chair. Ben Stone, who would question him, referred to his notes for a long moment before he stood and walked toward the witness.

"Mr. Smith, what is your occupation?"

"I own a small catering service," Smith replied.

"Where is that catering service located?"

"It's on Avenue of the Americas. I have a room in the basement of the Berry, Patmore and Daigh Building."

"Who are your principal customers?"

"My *only* customers are the people who work in that building."

"Do you have free access throughout the building?"

"Yes."

"How do the people who work there treat you?"

"They don't."

"That's a rather unusual answer, Mr. Smith. What do you mean by that?"

"I mean they don't treat me any way at all. Most of the time it's like I'm not even there. I'm a utility, like the water cooler, or the copy machine."

"Then what you are saying is that you enjoy a certain degree of invisibility, is that correct?"

"Yes."

"As a result of this invisibility, are you often privy to conversations which the participants would not otherwise want overheard?"

"Objection, Your Honor. The witness would have no way of knowing whether the participants would want the conversation overheard or not."

"Sustained."

"Let me reword that. Have you often overheard conversations in which you were neither the participant or the subject?"

"Yes."

"Have you heard the defendant in such conversations?"

"Yes."

"Would you share with the court, please, conversations you heard Eberwine having about JTJ Enterprises?"

"Objection, Your Honor. Where is this going?"

"Yes, Mr. Stone. Where is this going?" Judge Jones asked.

"Please bear with me a little longer, Judge," Stone replied. "I will establish the relevancy."

"I will allow you to proceed a bit further," Judge Jones said.

"Thank you, Your Honor. Mr. Smith, about JTJ Enterprises. You heard Mr. Eberwine in conversations dealing with them?"

"Yes."

"What was the nature of those conversations?"

"JTJ was the target of a hostile takeover,"

Smith said. "That's no secret now—it's been in the *Wall Street Journal* and other papers. Anyway, JTJ came to Berry, Patmore and Daigh to ask them to help fight off the takeover. Mr. Eberwine was given the task of becoming the white knight."

"Would you explain the term white knight?"

"That's a person who is armed with inside information which he can use to fight off the black knight, or hostile investor. He buys stock, either hoping to maintain control for the company or to drive the price of the stock up high enough to discourage the hostile attempt."

"Did Mr. Eberwine do what was expected of him?"

"No, sir. Mr. Eberwine not only provided the hostile buyer with that inside information, he used it to enrich his own portfolio."

"Objection, Your Honor. Mr. Eberwine's business ethics aren't the question."

"Bring it to a point, Mr. Stone," Judge Jones ordered.

"Your Honor, please bear with me a moment longer," Stone said. "I'm about there."

"I may have the wisdom of Solomon, but not the patience of Job," Judge Jones said. "Get there quickly."

"Yes, sir. Mr. Smith, was George Kinder aware of Eberwine's double-dealing?"

"Yes, he was."

"How do you know?"

"I overheard a conversation between the two," Smith said. "Mr. Kinder told Mr. Eberwine that the golden parachute had better be big enough for the both of them."

"What did he mean by that?"

"A golden parachute is the term used for the very generous bonuses paid to high-level executives when they leave a company. I believe Mr. Kinder was saying that he expected a very big bonus out of the deal, in exchange for his being quiet about it."

"Thank you, Mr. Smith," Stone said. "That is all."

Tom Henry stood then and walked around to the front of his table. He leaned back against the table and put his hands together, under his chin, as if in prayer. He stared at Smith for a long moment.

"White knight, black knight, hostile takeover, golden parachute. You are a veritable encyclopedia of information, Mr. Smith. How did you —a sandwich maker and coffee dispenser— learn so much about the stock market?"

"Well, I've been around it for several years now," Smith replied. "You pick things up."

"Yes, I heard how you pick things up," Henry said. "A little snooping here, some eavesdropping there, perhaps a few telephone calls piked, privileged notes read, that sort of thing."

"No," Smith replied. "Like I told the prosecutor, most of this stuff I just happened to overhear because—"

"Yes, yes, I know," Henry said, dismissing him with a wave. "Because you were invisible."

"Yes," Smith replied.

Henry walked over toward the jury and put his hands on the railing. He looked directly into the faces of the jurors.

"Oh, shit," Stone whispered under his breath. "I've seen this move before. Henry has something up his sleeve."

"Mr. Smith," Henry said, turning toward the witness, though continuing to stand in front of the jury box. "Did you notice that during your testimony I objected once or twice to procedural matters, but not once did I suggest that you don't actually enjoy this privilege of the invisible snoop? I did not challenge that because I know it is true. The reason I know it is true, Mr. Smith, is because I know that you have, for years, used this privileged and confidential information to enrich your own portfolio. You do own stock, don't you, Mr. Smith?"

"Yes."

"A great deal of stock?"

"I like to think I've invested well, over the years."

"Yes, and especially over the last three months. Is it not true, Mr. Smith, that, using the information you stole from Bart Eberwine, you have enriched yourself to the tune of four million dollars?''

There was a gasp of surprise from the courtroom, but it didn't go beyond that, so it was not necessary for Judge Jones to react.

"As I said," Smith replied quietly, "I like to think that I have invested well."

"You haven't always been so successful in your investing, have you?"

"Some investments pay off, some don't," Smith replied.

"What about those investments you made in 1969 and 1970? Are they examples of investments that didn't pay off?"

"Your Honor, I object," Stone said. "Where is this going?"

"Counselor, you have a reason for questioning this defendant about investments he made over twenty years ago?"

"I do, Your Honor," Henry said. "What I am attempting to do here is question the integrity of the witness. If I could find deceit in one area, I believe it would call into question his entire testimony."

"Very well, you may proceed."

"Thank you, Your Honor." Henry looked back at Smith, who was now staring at the floor.

"What about those investments in 'sixty-nine and 'seventy, Mr. Smith?"

"I'm not sure what investments you're talking about."

"Oh? Well, let me refresh your memory." Henry opened his briefcase and pulled out a stack of newspapers and magazines. "Let me read a few headlines for you," he said. He held up a newspaper. " 'Wall Street Whiz Kid Guilty of Fraud,' " he read. "Here's one. 'Thousands of Retired Americans Wiped Out by Retirement Fund Scam.' This one was on the cover of *Time* magazine about bankrupt retirees: 'Jonathan Sanford to retirees: Why are you crying? You are old enough not to believe in Santa Claus.' " Henry dropped the newspapers and magazines on the table so that they made a loud pop. He pulled out a videotape. "Of course, I have videotape here as well, interviews with a very arrogant young financial wizard who laughed at the misery of the thousands of men and women he had just defrauded . . . and in many cases ruined. But I don't need to show the tape too, do I . . . Mr. Sanford."

"My . . . my name is legally John Smith," Smith replied.

"It is now," Henry said. "But it was once Jonathan Sanford, am I right?"

"Yes," Smith admitted, quietly.

"The same Jonathan Sanford who defrauded thousands of hardworking men and women out of millions of dollars? Money that was supposed to let them grow old with dignity. Are you the same Jonathan Sanford, Mr. Smith?"

"I . . . I paid my debt to society," Smith said.

"By that, you mean you went to prison. But did you make any attempt to provide restitution for those who suffered as a result of your criminal activity?"

"No," Smith admitted. "Well, I really couldn't repay them, you understand. There was just too much money involved."

"And what happened to that money?"

"Some of it went to the government, some of it went to the families, and some of it was lost in bad investments."

"Thank you, Mr. Sanford."

"Objection, Your Honor. Defendant has already stated that his legal name is Smith."

Henry was halfway to his table when the objection was raised. He turned toward Smith and made an elegant, if sarcastic bow.

"Please forgive me for the mistake, *Mr. Smith,*" he said.

"Redirect, Mr. Stone?"

"Mr. Smith, have you in fact capitalized on information you overheard regarding JTJ stock?"

"I was not a principal," Smith replied. "There's no law against what I did."

Stone held up his hand. "Please, Mr. Smith,

just answer the question. Have you capitalized on information you overheard regarding JTJ stock?"

"Yes."

"Then it is safe to say that your interpretation of the information you overheard was correct?"

Smith, seeing then where Stone was going, smiled.

"Yes, I would say so."

"Have you any reason to believe your interpretation of the conversation you overheard between George Kinder and the defendant is less correct?"

"No reason at all. Kinder was definitely shaking down Eberwine."

"Thank you. No further questions."

"Very well, call your next witness, please."

After John Smith, there followed a virtual parade of prosecution witnesses. There were executives from JTJ whose testimony confirmed John Smith's accusation of unethical tactics on the part of Bart Eberwine. There were witnesses who testified that Bart Eberwine's normal disposition was one of compromise rather than confrontation, thus establishing the premise that his challenging, even baiting remarks to Ellis and Brown at the time of their confrontation, were so out of character for him that there had to be an ulterior reason for his behavior. There were doctors' reports stating that George

Kinder did die of knife wounds and not some other cause, and Clarence Ellis did die of gunshot wounds and not some other cause. A ballistics report matched the two bullets with the weapon Eberwine was carrying, and finally there was the videotape taken from the security camera. As the TV monitors were being put into place, Stone spoke to the judge.

"Your Honor, I would like to call Dr. Lynn Fielder to the stand to help interpret the tape."

"Objection, Your Honor," Henry protested immediately. "There are very few people in America now who have not seen that tape. It speaks for itself, there is no need for someone to interpret it for us."

"Your Honor, Dr. Fielder is a psychologist who specializes in body language," Stone explained. "Since the tape is without sound, the only way any of the participants can speak to us is by their body language."

Judge Jones played with his moustache for a long moment, then nodded in consent. "All right, Mr. Stone. I'm willing to listen to what your man has to say, once we establish his credentials to say it."

"Thank you, Your Honor. Dr. Fielder is a she. Prosecution calls Dr. Fielder to the stand."

Dr. Lynn Fielder was a tall, thin brunette with dark brown eyes and high cheekbones. Her glasses were horn-rimmed, with overly large round eyepieces. Her hair was tied back in a bun, as if she was deliberately trying to downplay what were actually very attractive features.

"Dr. Fielder, what is your educational background?"

"I graduated from the University of Chicago with a degree in psychology. I got my masters from Columbia, my doctorate from Harvard. I studied for a year at Vienna University in Vienna, Austria, and took part in the Goodings Seminar on body language and nonverbal communication in Geneva, Switzerland."

"And how are you currently employed?" Stone asked.

"I am, at present, the head of the Fielder Institute, an organization funded by grants from a consortium of businesses who use the information I provide."

"You have also done work for the police and the FBI, have you not?"

"I have."

"And what type service do you provide for them?"

"Sometimes in hostage situations I can interpret the body language of the hostage takers, or the hostages themselves, to provide the police with an estimate of what to expect from them. I've also been called to the scene of potential suicides, jumpers mostly, to determine the degree of likelihood that they will actually jump."

"How are you able to do this?"

"To one who can understand it, body language is fully one-half of a person's communication," Dr. Fielder explained. "Facial expressions, positions of the hands, arms, shoulders, even the angle of the body, provide us with these communication tools."

"But if everyone is not aware of how to interpret this language, how is it they can send the signals?"

Dr. Fielder smiled. "Those signals are an inherent part of our psyche," she explained. "Newborn infants, only an hour old, are already speaking in body language, and of course, for them, it is their only way of communication. I might add that there are very few parents who cannot understand the body language of their children."

Stone saw at least half a dozen people in the jury nodding in agreement with the witness, and he smiled in satisfaction. At least he would not have to sell them on the idea of body language . . . only on the meaning, as interpreted by Dr. Fielder.

"And finally, Dr. Fielder, you have written rather extensively on this subject, have you not?"

"Yes, I have written several papers and articles for various professional journals," she said.

"And two books, one of which, *People-speak*, became a best-seller."

"And you have testified as an expert witness in previous court cases?"

"Yes, several times."

"Your Honor, I ask that Dr. Fielder be declared an expert witness."

"Objections, Counselor?" Judge Jones asked Henry.

"No objections to Dr. Fielder's expertise, Your Honor. I'm well aware of her book, which was just three notches below mine on the best-seller list." Henry smiled at the doctor. "I just question the necessity of having the videotape interpreted at all."

"Yes, well, your objection was noted, Mr. Henry, and overruled. The court will allow Dr. Fielder to interpret the body language on the videotape in question. However, as it is very close to the noon hour and I do not wish to interrupt this witness in mid-testimony, we will recess until two o'clock this afternoon."

Chapter Eight

"**W**e took a pretty good blow this morning," Stone said during the noon recess. "Henry totally destroyed Smith's credibility." He snorted what might have been a laugh. "Or I guess I should say *Sanford's* credibility, since we can't even believe the guy's name."

"I can't believe we let something like that get by us," Wentworth said, sitting behind the desk in his office. "Jesus, I remember that case . . . all those old people carrying signs around in front of the courtroom. There's no telling how many lives Sanford ruined."

"And we were counting on him as our heaviest gun," Stone said. "I'll bet Tom Henry thought Christmas had come early this year. We were really suckered on that one.''

"Actually, it may not be as bad as you think," Robinette suggested.

"From behind what rainbow did you pull that optimistic observation?" Stone asked.

"I thought you recovered pretty well. I mean if believability is the only thing we're after, you established believability when you pointed out that Smith's use of the information to enrich himself does not detract from the truth of what he told us. On the contrary, it supported the believability of what he was telling us.''

"It may have reinforced believability, but not credibility," Stone said.

Robinette chuckled. "Come on, Ben, do you hear what you're saying? Believability? Credibility? That's the same thing.''

"No. There's a subtle difference," Stone insisted. "Believability has no synonyms, whereas credibility has such synonyms as character, decency, honesty, honor, principle, respect, and esteem. Admittedly, it's all a matter of perception, but our business is one of perception. People can believe a crook. But for someone to be credible, there has to be some redeeming quality to him. Unfortunately, after Henry got through with our witness this morning, he had no more redeeming tissue than a men's room cockroach.''

"All right, all right, I get the picture. But I still think you did a pretty good job of damage control."

"Maybe, but 'pretty good' is not good enough," Stone said. He turned to Wentworth. "Adam, we have to have that tape. The one Cerreta and Logan got from the FBI."

"I'm sorry, but that's not possible," Wentworth replied.

"But there *has* to be some way we can use it."

"Uh-uh," Wentworth said, shaking his head. "There's a federal order preventing it."

"Maybe we can go to another federal judge and get him to lift the order," Robinette suggested.

"That's not very likely."

"Well, can we at least let Cerreta and Logan use the tape to find some other source that has the same information as the tape?"

"You mean, start with the tape and work backward to validate it?" Wentworth asked.

"Yes."

Wentworth shook his head. "Why bother? It wouldn't stand up," he warned. "Once the court found out where we got our information to start with, the judge would throw it out. Remember, there's the problem of using the 'poisoned fruit of the forbidden vine.' "

"No, wait a minute!" Robinette said, holding up his hand. "Not really. The tape we heard is a legally obtained tape, therefore it isn't, technically speaking, poison fruit from a forbidden vine. We're only prevented from using it so as not to destroy a federal investigation in progress. And since the tape is legal, we have every right to use the information it contains, just so long as we don't disclose the source of that information."

"Paul's right, Adam," Stone said. "This isn't the same thing as illegally obtained evidence."

Wentworth thought for a moment, then nodded. "All right." He held up his finger in warning. "But tell Phil and Mike to be careful. If they do something to blow the feds' investigation, we're all going to wind up in the trick bag."

"I'll call them right now," Robinette offered.

"Don't take too long, we're due back in court," Stone said, checking his watch.

There were five TV monitors in use for the showing of the tape so that everyone in the courtroom had a clear view of the action on the screen.

"And now, Dr. Fielder, if you would, please, tell us what we are seeing," Stone began.

"Yes, of course," Dr. Fielder said. She had been polishing her glasses and she put them back on as the picture came on the screen.

"We'll start with the two men who are visible now."

"That would be Clarence Ellis, the bigger man on the left of the screen, and George Kinder, the smaller man to the right," Stone pointed out.

"Notice how loose the two men are," Dr. Fielder continued. "Their shoulders are relaxed. There is a fluid movement to their arms. And look at the hands. They're open, the fingers separated and slightly curled."

"What do such body attitudes tell us?" Stone asked.

"Well, quite clearly, that these two men are neither worried nor nervous. There is nothing here to indicate that a life-threatening situation is about to develop. Now, here, they have seen the defendant and Mr. Kinder leave the athletic club."

"Objection, Your Honor," Henry said. "Mr. Eberwine and Mr. Kinder are not on the screen. We have no way of knowing whether Ellis and Brown see them or not."

The tape was stopped.

"Your Honor, we, and our expert witness, have viewed this tape many, many times," Stone retorted. "She has already been established as an expert witness, without objection from defense. I believe her training and expertise qualifies her to make the judgment that Ellis and

Brown are, in fact, reacting to their first sight of Eberwine and Kinder."

"Objection overruled," Judge Jones said. "Restart the tape, please."

"Go ahead, Doctor," Stone invited.

"Yes," Dr. Fielder said. "Here, we can see that Ellis and Brown are reacting to their first sight of Eberwine and Kinder. As you can see there is a slight shifting of the shoulders, their arms are bent at the elbows, the movement of their hands a little more active. But overall their postures are still those of men who are confident and unafraid. But now, look. Do you see the sudden change? They're reacting to something Eberwine has said to them."

"Objection, Your Honor! We have no way of knowing that!" Henry called.

Again, the tape was stopped to allow the judge to consider the objection.

"Your Honor, I would again point out that Dr. Fielder has been declared expert at reading body language. If she says Ellis and Brown are reacting to something Eberwine said, we must accept that."

"Your Honor, we'll concede that her observation as to Ellis and Brown reacting to something is valid. But I object to her knowing just who they might be reacting to. Perhaps they are reacting to something said by Kinder."

"Objection as to who, specifically, they are

reacting to is sustained," Judge Jones said. He nodded, and the tape was restarted.

Dr. Fielder cleared her throat and continued her testimony. "Here," she said, "they are reacting to something that someone said. Notice how the shoulders grow tighter, their arms are drawn in, slightly, their hands not quite so loose. Notice, also, the legs, and particularly the feet. See how their knees are slightly bent, and how they have shifted their weight, coming up onto the balls of their feet. This is a classic confrontational mode.

"And now the other two gentlemen have entered the picture."

"Your Honor, for purposes of identification, that is George Kinder on the left and Bart Eberwine on the right," Stone noted.

"Thank you, Counselor," Judge Jones replied.

"Notice Mr. Eberwine's body language," Dr. Fielder continued. "He is in a far more advanced confrontational mode than either Ellis or Brown. His shoulders are so tight as to be bunched; his left hand, which is the only one visible here, is drawn into a very tight fist, and his head is thrust forward on his neck."

"And Mr. Kinder?" Stone asked.

"Mr. Kinder is showing shock and fear. He, clearly, is not in control of the situation, and it is frightening to him."

"Who *is* in control of the situation, Doctor?" Stone asked.

"At this point it is clearly Mr. Eberwine," Dr. Fielder said. "As you can see here, he is carrying the action and everyone else is reacting to him. And now, here comes the final confrontation. Mr. Brown has pulled a knife."

"To attack Eberwine and Kinder?"

"No," Dr. Fielder said, shaking her head. "I don't think so. I think, at this point, it is only a threatening gesture, a 'display' such as seen in the animal world when a cornered creature will make one last attempt at intimidation before actually attacking. Much like a dog, baring its fangs, and growling.

"And now, here is the denouement. Kinder steps between the two men, holding out some money. Even as he is doing so, Eberwine is taking his pistol out of the athletic bag. There is a brief scuffle and Kinder is stabbed. Immediately thereafter, Eberwine shoots, not the attacker, but the other man, who has ceased his own aggressive action and has become a shocked bystander."

"Let it be pointed out that the man Eberwine shot is Clarence Ellis," Stone said. "Dr. Fielder, do you believe that Clarence Ellis was Eberwine's target? Or was this incredibly poor shooting?"

Dr. Fielder shook her head. "No," she said.

"Ellis was clearly the target from the very moment Eberwine withdrew his pistol. If you would run the tape back, please? Just to the point where Eberwine draws his gun."

The tape was rewound to the point suggested, then replayed.

"Look at Eberwine's eyes," Dr. Fielder pointed out. "He is looking straight at Clarence Ellis, even though Ellis has no knife and, at this point, is not even particularly threatening."

"Why is he making Ellis his target, when Ellis is not threatening, but ignoring Brown, who is threatening?" Stone asked.

Dr. Fielder shook her head. "I can interpret action through body language," she explained. "But not the motive for that action. I know only that Ellis was Eberwine's intended target. I don't know why."

"Thank you, Doctor. Your witness, Mr. Henry."

Tom Henry got up from his chair and walked over toward the witness. "Tell me, Dr. Fielder," he began. "Are there many who are expert in your field?"

"It isn't a crowded field," Dr. Fielder replied. "But there are others."

"You say it isn't a crowded field. In fact, it is rather an obscure field, isn't it? With very little relevancy to the average person?"

"No, that isn't true at all," Dr. Fielder said.

"Anyone who has ever seen a stage play, or movie, or television drama, has benefited from body language. Directors of drama call the body language of their actors and actresses 'blocking,' and this blocking plays a very significant part in helping to establish the identity and personality of the characters they play."

"If I brought in one of my own expert witnesses, Doctor, might he or she disagree with your interpretation of the body language on this tape?"

Dr. Fielder shook her head. "No," she said. "At least not significantly."

"But there may be subtle differences?"

"Perhaps," Dr. Fielder agreed.

Tom Henry smiled broadly. "But Dr. Fielder, isn't that what this whole thing is? A discussion of subtleties? I mean, a subtle difference in this case might be significant, mightn't it?"

Dr. Fielder shook her head. "No," she said. "Not in the way you imply. It would not change the fact that Mr. Eberwine's aggressive action was the catalyst for everything that happened."

"I see," Henry replied. He stroked his chin. "But you did state, did you not, that while you can interpret action, you cannot interpret motive for those actions?"

"That is correct."

"So if my client is, as you say, leading the way

here, you have no way of knowing why he is doing so?"

"That is also correct."

"Isn't it possible then, Doctor, that what we are seeing here is exactly what my client had planned, what in fact he has admitted to? What if the plan was to create a confrontation whereby Ellis and Brown would appear to be menacing? What if the plan was for Eberwine to then step into the picture and run Ellis and Brown away—at gunpoint, if need be—in order to engender Kinder's gratitude? Would these pictures we have been watching be consistent with such a plan?"

"Well, that's very speculative, but—"

"Hold it, Doctor," Henry interrupted. "Isn't this whole thing speculative? That's why we have you appearing as the expert witness, isn't it? Because you have the skills to make such speculations?"

"Yes, I suppose so," Dr. Fielder admitted.

"Then is a hypothesis such as the one I just advanced—one in which Bart Eberwine purposely goads Ellis and Brown so as to create a tense atmosphere, only to step in and save the day before anything happens—isn't that a possible interpretation of what we have just seen?"

"Yes," Dr. Fielder admitted. "That might be one interpretation."

"Thank you, Doctor. No further questions."

"Redirect, Mr. Stone?"

"Yes, Your Honor," Stone said. "Dr. Fielder, when you were given the tape to study, you were told of the defense's claim that this was all staged, were you not?"

"Yes."

"So Mr. Henry's revelation that there might be another interpretation is not a bolt out of the blue, is it?"

"No."

"And yet, given that claim, you spent a lot of time analyzing the tape and came up with a scenario that is contrary to the defense claim, did you not?"

"I did."

"And what is the basis for your belief?"

"In studying the faces . . . and body language, of Ellis and Brown, it is clear that what happened there in the parking lot went far beyond their original expectations. If this was all part of some plan, the plan was clearly derailed by Mr. Eberwine's actions."

"Thank you, Doctor. No further questions."

"Thank you, Dr. Fielder, you may step down," Judge Jones said. "It is now three-thirty," the judge continued. "I have an appointment at four that I cannot reschedule. Therefore, if there are no strenuous objections, this court will stand adjourned until ten o'clock tomorrow morning."

Judge Jones struck his gavel, then Stone and Robinette began assembling their papers.

"So?" Robinette asked.

"So what?"

"What do you think? Did we gain any ground?"

Stone shook his head. "I don't know. He made mincemeat of Smith's testimony this morning and he muddied up Fielder's interpretation of the tape. It's going to be hard to nail the squirmy bastard."

Robinette laughed.

"What is it?" Stone asked.

"I'm not really sure who the squirmy bastard is you're talking about, whether it's Bart Eberwine or Tom Henry."

Stone grinned. "Neither am I," he admitted. He sighed. "I just hope Cerreta and Logan can come up with something to help."

Logan punched the off button on the tape player and sighed.

"Jeez, I don't know," he said. "I've listened to the damn thing so many times now, I can recite it by heart. But I don't have the slightest idea of where to start to find outside verification."

"Let's listen again," Cerreta said, rewinding the tape.

"Sure, why not?" Logan replied. He stood up and stretched. "What time is it, anyway?"

"Ten forty-five."

"Ten forty-five? Damn, we've spent half the night listening to this thing. You want some more coffee?"

"Yeah, thanks."

Logan walked over to the service counter to pour two more cups of coffee. The cleaning service was working, and he had to step around the woman who was pushing a vacuum cleaner. He was halfway back to his desk when he stopped and looked back toward the cleaning woman. He pursed his lips in thought, then continued on to the desk.

"You know, I've been thinking," Cerreta said. "If the FBI has a tape of this, I wouldn't be surprised if the mob didn't have one as well."

Logan chuckled. "Yeah, so what will we do, go to the mob and say, 'Excuse me, guys, but the nasty old FBI won't let us use a tape they made of one of your phone calls, so we were wondering if we could use yours?'"

"Not exactly," Cerreta replied, laughing with him. "But if there *is* another tape around, this thing isn't as tight as the FBI would want us to believe. Someone else knows of this call."

"Yeah, but who."

"There's that damn sound again," Cerreta said as a whining noise appeared in the background on the tape. "I wonder if the lab could take that out so we could hear better."

"Maybe," Logan said. He brought the coffee cup to his lips, then turned to look back at the cleaning lady again. "Wait a minute," he said. "Run that back."

"Run what back? Did you hear something?"

"You're damn right I did. Run it back to where the whine starts."

Cerreta ran it back a short piece, then started the tape again.

"Listen," Logan said.

"All right. Let me see if I can tune out the side noise."

"No! That's what I want you to listen to."

"Why would I—" Cerreta started to say, then seeing the smile on Logan's face and the direction his partner was looking, he stopped and listened to the sound as well. "It's a vacuum cleaner!"

"It's a lead-pipe cinch Eberwine wasn't running a vacuum," Logan said.

"No, but somebody was."

"And whoever that somebody was would have been as invisible as John Smith."

The double glass doors to the Berry, Patmore and Daigh Building were locked, but the security guard could be seen sitting behind his round desk in the well-lighted lobby. Cerreta knocked on the door, but the guard, who was drinking coffee and reading a newspaper, just looked up and waved his hand back and forth, as if saying that the place was closed and he had no intention of unlocking the doors.

"Open the door, damn it!" Cerreta shouted, banging again, louder this time. When the guard looked up again, both Cerreta and Logan were holding their badge folders up to the glass door. That, at least, had the effect of causing the guard to get up from his chair and walk over to the doors.

"What do you want?" he called through the doors.

"Police, we're on an investigation," Cerreta said. "Let us in."

The guard leaned over to get a closer look at the badges, sliding his glasses up his nose as he did so. Finally he nodded, then opened the door and stepped back.

"Sorry about that," he said as Logan and Cerreta came in. "But you can't be too careful these days."

"That's all right," Cerreta said. He walked over to the directory and found Eberwine's name, then turned back toward the guard. "Is there a cleaning team on the fourteenth floor?"

"Yeah, I think so," the guard said. "Let me check the register, I don't think they've checked out yet." He ran his finger down the sign-in and sign-out book.

"Wait a minute," Cerreta said. "Can I have a look at that book?"

"Well, yeah, I guess so," the security guard said. "I mean, I don't guess you need a warrant or anything."

"Thanks," Cerreta said. He started turning the pages back. "Mike, what was the date of that tape?" he asked.

"May twenty-third, 10:32," Logan replied.

"Here it is," Cerreta said. "Eberwine signed out at 10:45."

"That means he made the call from here."

"Let's go upstairs," Cerreta said.

There were six people working on the fourteenth floor, running vacuum cleaners, cleaning windows, emptying wastebaskets, and wiping down desks. When the two policemen stepped into the large bay area, the worker nearest them came over.

"Can I help you?" she asked, pushing a clump of hair back from her forehead. Her eyes were large, liquid-brown, and heavily lashed. They were pretty and expressive, though they shined out from a dark brown face that was already aging faster than the woman's years.

"I hope you can," Cerreta said, showing his

badge. He pointed to Eberwine's office. "Who normally cleans that office?"

"That would be Shelly," the woman said. "She handles all the offices on that side of the floor."

"Is she here?"

"Yes, I think I just saw her go into Mr. Jack's office. It's the third one from the end."

"Thanks," Cerreta said.

Shelly was running the vacuum cleaner when Cerreta and Logan stepped inside. Cerreta called to her and she turned the cleaner off, then looked at them curiously.

"Excuse us for bothering you. I'm Sergeant Cerreta, this is Detective Logan."

"Oh, my God! Has something happened to my baby?" Shelly gasped, putting her hand to her mouth.

"No, no! Nothing like that!" Cerreta said quickly, trying to calm her fears. "We just want to ask you a few questions, that's all."

"Questions? About what?"

"About Bart Eberwine."

Shelly laughed. "Are you serious? You want to ask me about Bart Eberwine?"

"Quite serious."

"Mister, I don't know what you think you goin' to get out of me. I ain't nothin' but a cleanin' woman. Eberwine don't even know I'm alive."

"Have you ever seen him?"

"Sure, a few times. He's been up here while we're working."

"Has he ever spoken to you?"

"About what?"

"About anything? How are you doing? How's the family? What do you think about the Mets?"

"What are you talkin' about?" she asked. "I don't think he's ever even seen me."

"Has he ever made any telephone calls while you were in his office?"

"A few."

"Can you hear what he's saying?"

Shelly nodded. "If we're in there workin' we can. It ain't like we're eavesdroppin' or anything. You can't help it."

"Good, good. Now, we're particularly interested in a call he made on the night of the twenty-third of May. Do you recall anything about—"

Shelly started shaking her head before Cerreta could even finish his question.

"My baby was born on May twenty-second," she said. "I was off work for a week."

"Who took your place?"

"I don't think nobody did. I think they just filled in for me."

Cerreta sighed, then looked over at Logan. "Okay, Mike," he said. "You start at this end, I'll start at the other. We'll talk to them all."

Twenty minutes later, with no results from their investigation, Cerreta and Logan started to leave. They were just about out when Shelly came over to them.

"I don't know if you'd be interested in talking to her," she said, "but my cousin Mabel used to work with us. She didn't leave until the middle of June, so she was probably here that night."

"Yes, thank you, we're very interested," Cerreta said. "Where can we find her?"

"You don't have to go too far. She's the team chief up on the sixteenth floor."

"Thanks," Cerreta said, smiling at her. "Thanks a lot."

"Yeah," Mabel said, leaning against the desk as she talked to Cerreta and Logan. "I did hear somethin' kind of screwy that night." Mabel turned and shouted toward one of the workers in the back of the room. "Shaneeka. Shaneeka, don't forget to do the blinds in Mr. Adams's office. He complained about it this morning, said they hadn't been done in a month."

"Well, he can complain all he want. I done 'em just last week," a young woman answered.

"Do them again," Mabel ordered. "And do them so he knows they're done."

"What's he doin' worryin' about blinds anyway?'' Shaneeka mumbled as she went into the office to take care of the job.

"What do you mean, screwy?" Cerreta said.

"I read the papers," Mabel said. "I know this Eberwine person is being tried for murdering Kinder, right?"

"Yes."

"Well, if Kinder had been killed by fallin' out a airplane, I coulda tol' you for sure you had the right man."

"Why do you say that?"

"'Cause I heard him on the phone sayin' somethin' about fixin' a parachute so that it don't open. Only, that ain't how it happened, is it?"

Cerreta smiled broadly. "Maybe it did," he said.

"What you mean?"

"It's a figure of speech. Do you remember what he said?"

"I remember exactly what he said," Mabel replied.

Cerreta opened his eyes wide in surprise. "How can you be so sure you remember it exactly?"

"'Cause I done tol' you, I thought it was kind of screwy talk. I mean, it ain't ever' night you hear someone talkin' about fixin' a parachute so it don't open, now, is it? Wouldn't you remember somethin' like that? 'Specially if your boy was a paratrooper?"

"I suppose I might," Logan agreed. "The question is, why haven't you told anyone about this before now?"

"Why should I?" Mabel replied. "Whatever it was Eberwine was talkin' about that night didn't happen. Kinder wasn't killed in no parachute accident. He got hisself cut. I figured I was better off keepin' myself out of it."

When the phone rang at two A.M., Ben Stone knocked a lamp over, then pushed the phone itself onto the floor, reaching for it. He finally picked the receiver up from the floor and mumbled into it.

"This had better be damn good," he said.

"Oh, I think it is, Ben, I think it is," Cerreta replied. He chuckled. "Anyhow, what do I care? You're the one snug in your bed while Logan and I are running all over Hell's half acre finding you another witness."

Stone sat up and ran his hand through his hair. "Did you say looking for, or finding?"

"Finding," Cerreta said. "I've got someone who can give you Eberwine's side of that telephone conversation."

"Who?"

"Her name is Mabel Applewhite. She works

256

on the cleaning team for Berry, Patmore and Daigh."

"Have her in the courtroom at nine o'clock tomorrow," Stone said. "Oh, and Phil?"

"Yeah?"

"You can wake me for this anytime."

Cerreta laughed. "Yeah, but will you respect me in the morning?" he teased.

Chapter Nine

Judge Jones gaveled the court into session at ten A.M. and instructed the state to call its next witness.

"Your Honor, prosecution calls Ms. Mabel Applewhite to the stand," Robinette said.

"Objection, Your Honor. Ms. Applewhite's name was not on the list of witnesses provided by the prosecution," Henry said.

"Your Honor, we only learned of the significance of the testimony of this witness very late last night," Robinette responded. "We faxed the information to Mr. Henry's office at nine o'clock this morning."

"Your Honor, approach the bench?" Henry asked.

"You may."

Henry, Robinette, and Stone stepped up to the judge's bench for the side bar.

"Prosecution faxed this information to me one hour ago, Your Honor. I certainly haven't had time to digest the information in one hour."

"Your Honor, I read the witness's testimony for the first time at seven o'clock this morning," Stone said. "That means we've had it only two hours longer than the defense."

Judge Jones stroked his chin. "Is it new testimony, Mr. Stone? Or is it a rehash of testimony we have already heard?"

"It is new testimony, Your Honor."

"What is it about?"

"Our witness is a cleaning lady in the office building where Eberwine worked. She overheard one side of a telephone conversation in which, I believe, Eberwine discussed the murder of Kinder."

"I don't see that in the material you gave me," Henry said.

"It's a matter of interpretation of the material," Stone said. "Prosecution would like to present it for the jury's consideration. Mr. Henry, of course, will be able to attempt to persuade the jury to see it differently."

"I don't like ambushes, Mr. Stone," Judge Jones said.

᾽ "No, sir, nor do I," Stone replied. "I assure you, Judge, we weren't holding this witness back. We didn't discover her until last night."

"All right, I am going to recess for the rest of the morning and reconvene at two o'clock this afternoon. At that time I will allow the witness to testify. Mr. Henry, that will give you longer to consider the witness and her testimony than prosecution has had up until now. Can you live with that?"

"Yes, Your Honor."

"Very well, return to your tables and I'll declare recess."

Mabel Applewhite was sworn in immediately after court reconvened. Robinette handled the cross-examination.

"Are you employed, Ms. Applewhite?" Robinette asked.

"Yes, I'm employed."

"And what is the nature of your employment?"

"I'm a cleaning-team leader for Patterson's Overnight Cleaning Service."

"And where do you work?"

"In Manhattan, the Barry, Patmore and Daigh Building on Avenue of the Americas."

"Were you working on the night of May twenty-third of this year?"

"I was."

"And on that night, did you clean Mr. Bart Eberwine's office?"

"I did."

"Was Mr. Eberwine present that night?"

"He was."

"Ms. Applewhite, did you overhear a telephone conversation between Bart Eberwine and another party that night?"

"I heard Mr. Eberwine's side of the conversation," she replied.

"Was there anything about the conversation you found strange?"

"There sure was."

"Would you share with the court what you found strange about that conversation?"

"The first thing I hear Mr. Eberwine say is, 'Kinder wants a parachute.' That get my attention, you see, 'cause my boy Travis, he's in the army in the Eighty-second Airborne. He jump out of airplanes in parachutes, so I figure I'll listen to what Mr. Eberwine is talkin' about." She looked over at the defendant. "Then I hear Mr. Eberwine say they is some kind of a problem. He say if Kinder don't get what he wants, he might start talkin' and that would ruin ever'thing. He say Kinder is askin' for a lot of money. Then after that he say to whoever he's talkin' to, 'I want you to fix it so his parachute don't open.' " Mabel pulled herself up straight. "Well, I take notice of that, you understan', 'cause I don't mind tellin' you, one of the things most scare me 'bout my boy bein' in the paratroopers is, I think all the time what would I do if that boy's parachute don't open when he jump? It scare me, so I don't like to think none about it, so when Mr. Eberwine say he want to fix it so Mr. Kinder's parachute don't open, I knew right away he was talkin' 'bout somethin' real bad.''

"Do you recall anything else he said?" Robinette asked.

"Only one more thing," she replied. "He said, 'I tol' you, I want you to fix it so his parachute don't open. I want you to make him go away.' Then he say, 'This ain't my field.'"

"Thank you, Ms. Applewhite. No further questions, Your Honor."

"Mr. Henry?" Judge Jones invited.

Tom Henry stood up. "Ms. Applewhite, what is a golden parachute?"

"A what?"

"A golden parachute. Have you ever heard that term?"

"I guess it be a parachute that be gold color," she replied.

"Do you know what the term 'green mail' means?"

"No, sir."

"What about churning, LIFO, triple witching hour? Do you know what any of that means?"

"Your Honor, I object," Robinette said. "We didn't put this witness on as an expert in stock market terminology."

"Your Honor, I'm only pointing out the fact that there are certain terms that Ms. Applewhite does not understand, therefore she may very well have misinterpreted Mr. Eberwine's perfectly innocent conversation."

"Objection overruled," Judge Jones said.

"No further questions, Your Honor."

"Does prosecution have any further witnesses?"

"None, Your Honor," Stone said. "Prosecution rests its case."

"Defense, you may present your case."

"Your Honor, at this time I would request a directed verdict," Henry said, "based upon the fact that prosecution has totally failed to prove its case."

"Thank you for your suggestion, Counselor," Judge Jones replied. "But I think I shall let the jury hear the case. You may proceed."

"Defense calls to the stand Bart Eberwine."

Eberwine took the oath then sat in the witness chair.

"Mr. Eberwine, you are aware that you don't have to testify, are you not?"

"Yes," Eberwine replied. "I am aware of that."

"In fact, I suggested that the prosecution's

case is so weak that you wouldn't have to testify, but you requested that I put you on the stand. Is that also a correct statement?"

"That is correct."

"Why did you wish to testify?"

"I don't want to win this case by default," Eberwine replied. "I want the jury to know—I want the world to know—that I am innocent of poor George Kinder's death. I want them to hear my side of the story."

"Very well, Mr. Eberwine, let's hear your side of the story," Henry said. "Now, do you admit to contacting Mr. Turner to make arrangements for Clarence Ellis and Teroy Brown to show up at the parking lot of the Executive Stress Athletic Club?"

"Yes."

"Why did you do such a thing?"

Eberwine ran his hand through his hair and sighed. "I wish to heaven I had never done it," he said. "But I was trying to put together a package for JTJ in order to save the company from a hostile takeover bid. This was a very difficult situation with a great deal of money on the side of the black knight . . . more money, in fact, than JTJ had access to. In order to save them, I had to . . . bend the rules a bit."

"In bending these rules, would you be violating federal trade regulations?"

Eberwine sighed again. "When I am finished

with this trial, there is no doubt in my mind that I will have to face charges to that effect," he replied. "At this point I would like to decline to answer as to whether I would be violating any specific regulations. I will say, however, that the mechanism I put together to save JTJ was very complex, and I wasn't sure Kinder could understand exactly what I was doing. But whether he could understand or not, I did need his help in holding everything together. Because I was afraid he wouldn't understand, or appreciate, exactly what I was doing, I decided that the best way to ensure his cooperation and support would be to win his gratitude. I thought long and hard about how to do that, then I decided that the greatest gratitude one might have to another would be if one's life was saved by another. I therefore set about to make it appear as if I were saving George Kinder's life."

"By having Ellis and Brown attack you?"

"Yes. Well, no, not exactly," Eberwine said. "You see, I had never met them, so I didn't know, exactly, who was going to show up. When I saw them by the car, I assumed they were the people I had arranged for, but . . . when I started to put the game plan into effect, they didn't play according to the ground rules I had laid down."

"Game plan? Ground rules? Would you explain that, Mr. Eberwine?"

"Yes. You see, no one was supposed to be hurt. Neither Ellis nor Brown, and certainly neither one of us. You can imagine my surprise, then, when I saw Brown stabbing poor George."

"Mr. Eberwine, we watched the videotape together. You heard Dr. Fielder testify that, according to body language, you were dictating the events. Is that true?"

"Well, yes, it was supposed to be true," Eberwine replied. "But things got out of hand so quickly that I was no longer in charge. I'll tell you the truth, at the end there, I wasn't even sure these were the same two men I had hired. I mean, they were supposed to take all the verbal abuse I could heap upon them, then turn and leave. That was all part of the plan. There was nothing said, anywhere, about one of them going berserk and attacking us with a knife. The last thing I wanted to do was kill one of those men . . . let alone see my friend killed."

"So you emphatically deny that you desired Kinder's death, or that the killing was any part of some plan of yours?"

"I emphatically deny that," Eberwine said. "I am guilty of a tactical error . . . a tactical error with tragic consequences. I am, therefore, responsible for my friend's death in the same way the driver of a car is responsible for an accident which occurs through no fault of his own, in which someone is killed. But I am not guilty of premeditated murder."

"What about the telephone call that Ms. Applewhite referred to?"

"I have to be honest with you, I don't recall that specific telephone call, so I don't know who I was talking to. But my suggesting that I wanted it fixed so that Kinder's parachute wouldn't open, probably referred to my wanting to deny him a golden parachute so he would have to stay with us." Eberwine chuckled. "You know, it's actually a wonder she didn't hear me use the term 'poison pill.' If she had, she might have thought I was planning to poison someone."

"What is a poison pill?" Henry asked.

"It's a mechanism structured into a company to prevent it from being taken over, so that if a hostile buyer tries, he will, in fact, destroy the very company he is trying to buy. It is analogous to a spy with a cyanide capsule in his teeth. If he is captured, he bites down on the capsule, thus preventing the enemy from getting any information."

"Poison pill, parachutes that don't open, I guess your business is filled with terms that would be difficult for the uninitiated to understand," Henry suggested.

"Yes, it is, but I'm sure no more so than any other business with its own jargon."

"Thank you, Mr. Eberwine. I have no more questions. Your witness, Counselor."

Ben Stone approached the witness stand. "Mr. Eberwine, how much money, to date, have you made as a result of your stock manipulations with JTJ?"

"Objection, Your Honor, outside the scope of the direct examination," Henry protested.

"On the contrary, Your Honor. The amount of money Mr. Eberwine made in his manipulations goes to the heart of our case. We contend that protecting the money to be made on the JTJ deal was the motive for his killing George Kinder, and Defendant opened up a matter of the JTJ transaction on direct."

"Objection overruled."

"I have made a little over ten million dollars," Eberwine said.

"So Mr. Smith, the man whose testimony your lawyer tried to discredit, was correct in his estimate of your profit?"

"Yes."

"Mr. Smith knew how much money you were making. Who else knew? Did George Kinder know how much money you had made?"

"No."

"Why not?"

"Well, he had his portfolios to look after and I had mine."

"In fact, was anyone, other than Mr. Smith
aware of how much you were making?"

"No."

"Why not? Isn't there a system of accounting
How could you get such a windfall throug
without anyone knowing?"

"I . . . I didn't do it all through my com
pany," Eberwine said. "I spread it out throug
several companies."

"Did Kinder know you were dealing wit
other companies?"

"I don't know."

"If he had known, what would he have
done?"

"Any answer I might give you would be spec
ulative. I don't know what he would have
done."

"Mr. Eberwine, you testified that you wanted
to get Kinder's gratitude because you wanted
his support on a complicated business venture
What, exactly, was that venture?"

"There was no specific business venture.
What I said was that the mechanism I had put in
place to save JTJ was very complex and I
couldn't be sure that Kinder would understand
it. If anyone in the company started questioning
what I was doing, I wanted to be able to count
on Kinder's support, even if he didn't understand."

"If your . . . plan . . . had been success-

ul, do you think you could have counted on
Kinder's support?''

"Yes."

"Why?"

"Because George Kinder was a good friend
and a man who would honor his obligations.''

"And he would be obligated to you for saving
his life?''

"Yes."

"I see. Now, Mr. Eberwine, when your . . .
plan,'' as before, Stone set the word "plan"
apart from the rest of the sentence, "went into
operation, why is it that you did not see, sooner,
that things were going awry?''

"I don't know. I can't answer that question.''

"But you did see they were going awry, didn't
you? You did have your gun out before Kinder
was stabbed.''

"I . . . I know now that I did, because I have
watched myself on the tape, many times,''
Eberwine answered. "But I'm not indepen-
dently aware of that fact, and therefore I can't
comment on it.''

"In actual fact, things didn't go awry, did
they, Mr. Eberwine? In fact they went just as you
planned. You purposely chose the most challenging words and gestures to incite just the
reaction you got. Isn't that right, Mr.
Eberwine?''

"No, no. That's not it at all. I had no idea all

that was going to happen. I mean, once things started, it happened so fast that I . . . I didn't even know I was shooting until I startled myself by the sound of the gun going off.''

"That brings up another question that everyone has been asking, Mr. Eberwine. If you were shooting to protect your friend, why didn't you shoot the man who had the knife? Why did you shoot Clarence Ellis, who was just standing there as shocked as George Kinder by everything that was going on?''

"I don't know why I shot Clarence Ellis instead of Teroy Brown," Eberwine replied. "I thought I shot the man who killed George. I could have sworn that was the one I shot, right up until I saw otherwise on the tape.''

"And finally, Mr. Eberwine, why were you unable to identify Teroy Brown in the lineup, when other witnesses who were much farther away than you were able to do so?''

Eberwine shrugged. "I don't know. I guess when I saw him in the lineup it was so different from the way I saw him the first time that I just couldn't be sure. You know how it is if you see someone that you see often in a place other than where you're used to seeing them? Maybe it's something like that.''

"When you watched Teroy Brown testify here in court, did you recognize him then?''

"Yes.''

"Why is it you recognized him then, but not before?"

"I had time to think about it," Eberwine replied. "When you showed him to me in the lineup, you didn't give me time to think."

"You murdered George Kinder, didn't you?"

"No, I didn't."

"Oh, I think you did, Mr. Eberwine."

"Objection, Your Honor, counsel is badgering the witness."

"Sustained," Judge Jones said, glaring at Stone.

"Your Honor, I have no further use of this . . . this person," Stone said.

"Redirect?"

"No redirect, Your Honor," Henry replied.

"Call your next witness."

"No more witnesses, Your Honor," Henry said.

"Counselor, am I to believe that your entire case consists of one witness?" Judge Jones asked.

"Yes, Your Honor, the one witness—in fact, the *only* witness—who knows the truth about what actually happened," Henry answered. "I don't feel that any other witnesses are necessary. Prosecution took their best shot and didn't even come close to the mark. We're ready for summation and to turn it over to the jury. Defense rests."

Judge Jones looked up from his bench. "Gentlemen, due to the lateness of the hour . . . and the fact that I do not want to put any time constraints upon your closing arguments, I am going to adjourn court until ten A.M. tomorrow morning."

"The Applewhite testimony didn't work, Adam," Stone said in the D.A.'s office that evening. "She had only a partial account, that from one side, and it out of context."

"Henry shot big enough holes in her testimony to drive a truck through," Robinette added.

"I'm sorry," Wentworth said.

"We've got to have the tape."

"We'll never get it. Besides, it's too late now. Even if you did get it, I doubt if Judge Jones would let it in."

"So, what are we going to do? Let the guilty son of a bitch walk?" Robinette asked.

Wentworth smiled and shook his head. "Ben, do you remember the debating tourney at Columbia, your senior year in college?"

"Yes."

"I was one of the judges, remember? That was the first time I ever heard you speak. Tom Henry was your partner in that tourney, I believe. But I thought you were better. I knew then that you were going to be something."

"If you recall, as well, Adam, Tom Henry was the one who won the trophy for the most outstanding debator of the entire tourney."

"Oh, yes, I recall. Tom Henry was flamboyant, even then. But your organization of logic and fact was better . . . much better. I have no reservations about how you'll do tomorrow. When you go before the jury, you'll make them forget everything Tom Henry said."

"I wish I had your confidence," Stone said. "I mean to be able to say, without reservation, that we're going to win."

Wentworth smiled. "Yeah, well, or maybe we won't."

All three men laughed.

LAW &
ORDER

Chapter Ten

"**M**r. Henry, you may present your closing statement," Judge Jones said as soon as court was reconvened.

Tom Henry walked over to address the jury, but before he did so, he took his watch off and lay it on the corner of the banister.

"I always like to do this before I give any sort of talk," he said. "I find that it gives my audience a sense of comfort by providing the *illusion* that I am actually going to pay attention to time."

The jury laughed.

"Illusion," Henry said, holding up his finger. "That's a term with which we are all familiar. Let's talk about illusion for a moment. There are optical illusions, the illusions of magicians, the illusion of special effects in the movies." Henry smiled, then looked toward the prosecutor's table. "And, of course, there is that illusion woven by the prosecutors during the course of this trial . . . the bizarre illusion that Bart Eberwine, somehow, purposely set up this whole thing, subjecting himself to a mugging and possible death by stabbing, in order to have his friend killed."

Henry sighed and shook his head.

"Well, let's give credit where credit is due, ladies and gentlemen. Prosecution scores big on originality, big on bombast and oratory, and they are a couple of well-scrubbed, well-dressed fellows, so we'll even throw in a few points for neatness."

Again the jury laughed.

"But as to the illusion they're trying to create?" Henry held his hand out flat in front of him and tilted it side to side. "Ehh," he said. "Without special effects, only so-so."

There was another chuckle.

"Ladies and gentlemen, look at what they're trying to get you to believe. They're trying to get you to believe that Bart Eberwine set up a scenario whereby he had a man killed by someone else. Now, of course, murder for hire has occurred before, and that in itself might not be so unbelievable. In this case, however,

Eberwine is supposed to have used a third party to kill his friend, without the third party even being aware that he was being used! You heard Eberwine testify that no one was supposed to be hurt. You heard Edward Turner testify that no one was supposed to be hurt. You even heard the man who did the actual killing admit that his instructions were, *no one was supposed to be hurt*. And yet, with all this testimony coming from all the parties of the incident, the prosecutor has, somehow, come up with the theory that Eberwine intended, from the very beginning, for George Kinder to be killed.

"And what is the only shred of evidence they have to support that claim? They have the secondhand testimony of a cleaning lady who overheard *one half* of a telephone conversation . . . a conversation which was so laced with investment jargon that Eberwine may as well have been speaking in Japanese. Eberwine wanted to fix it so' that Kinder's parachute didn't open? Come on, give me a break.

"You know, ladies and gentlemen, when I was a boy, I was a big, big, fan of the Yankees, and when I couldn't get out to the park to see the games, or when I couldn't watch them on TV, I would listen to them on the radio. I remember one game when I was very, very young, where Mel Allen said, and I quote, 'The Yankees went down in the bottom of the fifth and Mantle died on third.' '' Henry paused for a moment. "When I heard that Mantle died on third, there was no consoling me. I cried my head off until my mother explained to me that my hero, Mickey Mantle, didn't actually die. That was merely baseball jargon, meaning that no one was able to drive Mantle in and thus he was left stranded on third base when the inning ended.''

Again there was laughter from the jury.

"I do not question the veracity of the witness, Mabel Applewhite. I'm sure she heard every word just as she described them to us. But I do suggest that she did not know what she was hearing.

"I do not even quarrel with the information provided by the other witnesses, even though they be convicted felons all. We do, however, take issue with the interpretation of the information they provided.

"And if you take issue with that interpretation . . . or even if you have a *shadow of a doubt* as to the prosecution's interpretation of that information, there is but one course open to you. You must find the defendant, Bart Eberwine, innocent of the charge of murder.''

Tom Henry retrieved his Rolex, slipped it on his wrist, then returned to his seat.

"Mr. Stone," Judge Jones said. "Your summation, sir?''

Ben Stone walked over and stood in front of the jury with both hands resting lightly on the railing.

"In testimony taken in this court during these proceedings, we heard from Bart Eberwine's own lips just how much money he has made through, and I quote his own words, 'bending the rules' of the business in which he works. The rewards of this rule-bending have been enormous. It is easy to see, then, how someone who has 'bent the rules' to make such an enormous amount of money would have an equal disregard for the rules in protecting it. If a person without ethics perceived such a threat, he would go to any means to eliminate either the threat or the source of that threat.

"George Kinder discovered Bart Eberwine's stock manipulations and approached him with the suggestion that he be included in the profits, implying that he would blow the whistle if Eberwine didn't comply.

"Eberwine did not wish to share any of his profits, so he made a telephone call to an outside source in which he discussed 'making the problem go away' . . . 'making him,' meaning Kinder, 'go away.' Then, after having discussed the situation with the unidentified party on the other end of the phone, Eberwine proceeded to do just that."

Stone held his hands in front of him, cupped,

as if they were surrounding a ball. "He did this by devising a murder that was so diabolically clever that there were no corners to get hold of . . . like a ball. Then he covered this ball with a patina of quicksilver. Around this ball of quicksilver, the defense has laid a mine field of jargon, designed to trip us up as we searched for the truth. Words like 'golden parachute' and 'poison pill.' " Stone shook his head slowly, and smiled. "We even heard a poignant little story of how Mickey Mantle died on third. All this is designed to make us believe that Mabel Applewhite did not hear what she knows she heard.

"You may ask how could Bart Eberwine discuss another man's murder so casually in front of a witness? Quite simply, ladies and gentlemen, because, in Eberwine's mind, he had no witnesses. Ms. Applewhite wasn't even there. You see, Bart Eberwine is one of those rich and powerful men who live in their own world, and who dehumanize anyone and everyone who does not meet their standards of importance. Mabel Applewhite wasn't a person with feelings, hopes, desires, and family. Mabel Applewhite was an ashtray.

"But you and I know that Mabel Applewhite isn't an ashtray. We have seen and heard her testify with confidence and dignity, and in chilling detail, about the telephone conversation she overheard. Of course, defense would have you believe that the conversation was so couched in stock market jargon that Mabel Applewhite didn't know what she was hearing. But Mabel Applewhite did *not* misunderstand the tone and tine of that conversation. Make no mistake about it, that was clearly a conversation in which Eberwine was discussing the murder of George Kinder.

"It could be, however, that you do have a shadow of doubt as to the interpretation of that telephone conversation. Perhaps there is even some doubt as to motive. I will grant you that. But there is one thing of which there can be *no* doubt. Ladies and gentlemen of the jury, George Kinder *was* killed.

"There can be no doubt as to *how* he was killed. *He was stabbed by Teroy Brown.*

"There can be no doubt as to *why* Teroy Brown was there. He was there because Bart Eberwine had paid money to have him there.

"There you have it, ladies and gentlemen, the *what,* the *how,* and the *why* of George Kinder's death, and *those facts are beyond a shadow of a doubt.*"

Stone put his hands together, prayerlike, just under his chin, then looked at the jury box, making eye contact with everyone there.

"Now, I'm going to tell you something." He separated his hands and held up a finger.

"Folks, it makes no difference what kind of smoke screen the defense puts up regarding motive, jargon, plans gone awry, or tragic accidents. Because the bottom line is *cause* and *effect*. The *cause* is action taken by Bart Eberwine. The *effect* of that action was George Kinder's death. It's that simple, ladies and gentlemen. *George Kinder is dead because of action taken by Bart Eberwine.*

"I have already told you that *I* believe Eberwine *intended* to kill Kinder. You may have a shadow of a doubt about that." Stone waved his hand. "Okay, hang on to your shadow of doubt, because *it doesn't matter whether he intended to kill Kinder or not.* Bart Eberwine is guilty . . . by his own admission . . . of murder by 'depraved indifference to human life.'

"I would like to read to you from *Penal Law,* Article 125, part 3, the passage dealing with *depraved indifference to human life.*"

Stone returned to his table and took the book, handed to him by Robinette, already open to the correct page. He cleared his throat and read aloud.

"The term 'depraved indifference to human life' is not easily defined. It refers to a particularly egregious form of wantonness, of lack of concern for human life, that makes a person's conduct 'equal in blameworthiness to intentional murder.' Intentional murder and depraved indifference murder are both class A felonies, punishable by a maximum term of life imprisonment. Examples of depraved indifference are: firing a gun three times in a packed bar room, continually beating a young child over a five-day period, placing a time bomb in a public place, opening the door of a lion's cage in a zoo."

Stone slapped the book closed with a loud pop, then handed it back to Robinette.

"Ladies and gentlemen, I submit to you that when Bart Eberwine hired two violent men, indeed, set out to hire them because they *were* violent men, he released the latch to the lion's cage in the zoo. And when they showed up at the parking lot, by his arrangement, and he began inciting them to violence with racial slurs and challenging remarks, *he swung that door open*.

"There is no doubt about these facts, ladies and gentlemen. Forget about motive, forget about intent, Bart Eberwine murdered George Kinder by an act of depraved indifference to human life. Viewed in that light, our task becomes easier, and more clear. We can, and we must, find him guilty."

When Stone sat down, Robinette slid a little piece of paper toward him. "I don't care what the jury decides," the paper read. "In my book, you kicked his ass."

Stone smiled, then wadded the paper up and stuck it in his jacket pocket. They listened as the judge charged the jury, then adjourned the court.

Tom Henry walked over to the prosecutor's table with a big smile on his face and his hand extended.

"Fantastic job, Ben," he said. "I'd almost forgotten how good you are." He rubbed his hands together as he watched the gallery file out of the courtroom. "God, it's great to be a lawyer when you have a case like this, don't you think? I mean, we went head to head and toe to toe slugging it out. We both took some pretty damaging hits . . . and I'm not sure but that you didn't dish out a little more than you took. But it doesn't matter now, it's all out of our hands." He nodded toward the jury, which was, at that moment, being led away by the bailiff. "It's funny, isn't it? The best legal minds in the country try the case, but in the final analysis the decision will be rendered by ribbon clerks and mechanics, taxi drivers and accountants, school teachers and insurance salesmen. People who never heard a precedent, or ever read one word of law." He sighed. "There ought to be a better way."

"I'm not ready to scrap the system," Stone replied.

"No, I'm not either," Henry said quickly.

'Don't get me wrong. I just think there ought to be a better way, that's all. Could I buy you fellas a cup of coffee while we wait?''

"Thank you, no," Ben said. "We've let a pile of work grow . . . this might be a good time to take care of it."

"I know what you mean," Henry said. "Well, I'll see you when the jury comes back in."

"We've got this one, Ben. Even Henry thinks you beat him," Robinette said as he and Stone returned to their office.

"I wish I shared your confidence," Stone replied. "But I believe Henry has something up his sleeve."

"What makes you think so?"

"It's just a feeling I have," Stone said. "It's like he knows something that I don't know."

"Whatever it is, it's too late now," Robinette said. "The case has gone to the jury . . . we'll have a decision before the day is out, and in my opinion, it will be guilty."

It took less than two hours for the jury to come to a decision, and less than thirty minutes for Stone and Robinette to return to the courtroom. Henry and Eberwine were already at their table when Stone and Robinette sat down. Henry smiled and nodded at Stone; Stone returned the nod, but not the smile.

"The defendant will rise, and face the jury," Judge Jones said.

Eberwine stood and, as directed, looked toward the jury.

"Would the foreman please stand?" the bailiff asked.

From the end seat in the first row of the jury box, a short, stout, gray-headed woman stood.

"Have you reached a verdict?" Judge Jones asked.

"We have, Your Honor," the woman answered in a clear, strong voice. Stone remembered that she was a history teacher in junior high school.

"To the charge of murder in the second degree, how do you find the defendant?"

"We find the defendant guilty, Your Honor," the foreman answered.

Stone glanced over at Eberwine to check his reaction. He never batted an eye.

"What a cool son of a bitch you are," he said, so quietly that only Robinette could hear him.

"So say you all?" the judge asked the foreman.

"So say we all, Your Honor."

"Thank you very much, Madam Foreman, ladies and gentlemen. The jury is excused. Counselor for the defense, sentencing will be at two o'clock in the afternoon, Thursday next."

"Thank you, Your Honor," Henry said.

"Court is adjourned," the judge said, slapping the gavel hard on the pad.

Cerreta and Logan were the first two to offer their congratulations to Stone and Robinette. That was followed almost immediately by other police officers and members of the prosecuting attorney's staff. Stone and Robinette smiled, shook hands, and exchanged pleasantries, but Stone couldn't turn his attention away from Tom Henry. The defense attorney did not have the look of a man who had just lost a major case . . . and Stone didn't like that. He didn't like it one bit.

"Ben," Robinette said, sticking his head in through Stone's door. "Something's up. Wentworth wants to see us." It was three weeks after the verdict had been handed down.

"What is it?" Stone asked.

"They've just overturned Eberwine's conviction."

"What? Why?"

"I'm not sure."

Adam Wentworth was sitting back in his chair with his arms folded across his chest when Stone and Robinette arrived.

"What is it, what's wrong?" Stone asked. "That was a good conviction, how could it be overturned?"

"Lack of disclosure," Wentworth said, leaning forward to slide a piece of paper across the desk toward Stone.

Stone picked it up and began reading. "What?" he asked, looking up. "What do they mean we didn't disclose the fact that we had a copy of a tape? We didn't use the tape."

"No, but we used information from it," Wentworth said. "That was how we tracked down Mabel Applewhite, remember?"

"So what? Her testimony was virtually useless."

"Nevertheless, we had information we did not disclose. On motion for a new trial, the judge decided that it gave prosecution an unfair advantage."

Robinette moaned. "How can he do that?"

Wentworth chuckled. "Come on, Paul, you know better than that. He's a judge. He can do just about anything he wants."

"Son of a bitch!" Stone said. "We had him nailed!"

Wentworth scratched his chin. "Yeah, well, he's not getting off scot-free. The feds are after him now."

"We get him first, don't we? For retrial?"

Wentworth shook his head. "I'm afraid not. We've cut a deal with the federal prosecutor. It's part of a plea bargain. The federal charges against him will be dropped. He's going to co-operate fully with the FBI in getting Costaconti, then he'll go immediately into the federal witness protection program. Without his ill-gotten gains, I might add."

"A lot of good that does us," Stone growled.

"Come on, Ben, it's not that bad of a deal when you think about it. Angelo Costaconti is one of the two or three top mobster bosses in the entire country. I mean, he's done things that makes Eberwine seem like he was playing in the minor leagues. I'm as anxious to get him off the streets as the feds are, and if we had a hand in bringing this around, I'm proud of it. What difference does it make how we did it?"

"Yeah, I guess you're right," Stone said.

"And look at it this way," Robinette added. "We beat Henry. The jury returned a guilty verdict."

Stone smiled. "Yeah, we did beat him, didn't we?"

"Oh, by the way, Henry and Eberwine are holding a press conference on the courthouse steps at eleven," Wentworth said. "I just tell you that in case you would care to catch it."

"I'm on your side in this," Joanna Blaylock said to Cerreta and Stone as they stood on the courthouse steps. She brushed back a fall of hair.

"Yeah? What side is that?" Cerreta asked.

"Well, your investigation discovered that

Eberwine was guilty, the prosecutors proved that Eberwine was guilty, the jury found him guilty, yet the court system let him go on some technicality.''

"Uh-huh," Cerreta said laconically. "Nevertheless, you are down here to cover the news conference."

"He is news, Sergeant. And it is my job," she replied.

"Have you ever thought that perhaps your job makes our job harder?" Cerreta asked.

"Are you proposing censorship?"

Cerreta shook his head. "No, not censorship," he said. "But perhaps a little responsibility would be nice."

"I don't make the rules of life, Sergeant, I just live by them," Blaylock replied.

"Don't we all?"

"I have to get over there, my cameraman is set up."

"You do that," Cerreta replied.

Stone and Robinette arrived at the courthouse steps just as Joanna Blaylock was walking away from the two detectives.

"Another interview, Phil?" Stone asked with a chuckle.

"I told her to see my agent," Cerreta replied. "You two come down here to catch the show?" he asked.

"Yeah, to watch Henry gloat," Stone an-

swered. "I guess there's that much of a maso-
chist in me."

"What do you mean, gloat? You whipped his
ass, he's got nothing to gloat about," Logan
said.

"Yes he does. He got the conviction overturned and the charges dropped. That was what
he was hired to do, and that's what he did."

"Well, Eberwine's not home free. The feds
are going to squeeze him for every ounce,"
Cerreta said.

Halfway down the steps, Joanna Blaylock, as
well as a phalanx of video, audio, and print
reporters were gathered around Tom Henry
and Bart Eberwine.

"My client will make a statement," Henry was
saying, "then he'll answer any questions you
may have."

Eberwine stepped up to the microphones.
"First of all, I want to thank Tom Henry for his
tireless effort on my behalf. I also would like
to . . ."

"Hey, Phil," Logan said. "Look at that guy
there. Isn't that—"

"Paulie Sangreo," Cerreta answered for him.
"What's he doing here?"

"Oh, shit!" Logan said, starting down the
steps toward Sangreo. The reason for his exple-
tive was that Sangreo had just pulled a pistol

from under his jacket and was moving, quickly, toward Eberwine, who didn't see him.

"Eberwine! Look out!" Cerreta shouted.

The warning was too late. There were two loud pops, then screams and shouts from the crowd of reporters who, dropping cameras and recorders, began running. Sangreo turned away and began running back down the steps. A car with the back door open and its engine running was waiting just by the curb. Logan and Cerreta, their own guns drawn, had an interception angle on him, with a good chance of cutting him off.

"Hold it, Sangreo!" Cerreta shouted.

Sangreo, who had not seen the pursuing policemen until that very moment, stopped, then raised his gun and fired at them.

Both Logan and Cerreta returned fire, shooting only one shot each; but that was enough. Sangreo pitched backward, then fell on his back down the stone steps. His gun clattered all the way down to the sidewalk.

The driver of the car accelerated quickly, and though both Logan and Cerreta ran down to the street, they did not have a clear line of fire and had to watch in frustration as the car, with the number on its license plate obscured by mud, drove away. When they returned to look at Sangreo, his eyes were open, but already growing opaque in death. There were two bullet holes in his chest.

"Damn!" Cerreta said. "Damn, I hate it when something like this happens."

"What about Eberwine?" Logan asked. He looked up and saw several people gathered around the body, which, like Sangreo, was sprawled on the concrete steps. Logan caught Robinette's eyes, and, with a slight nod, he questioned him.

Robinette shook his head slowly.

"Eberwine is dead," Logan said.

"I wonder how much money he has in his pocket?" Cerreta asked.

"What?"

"They say he made ten million bucks out of his scheme," Cerreta said. "What good is it now?"

In the distance they could hear the sound of the approaching ambulance.

A BRUTAL MURDER . . .

The body of a homeless woman is found beneath the rubble of a demolished building in Midtown Manhattan. N.Y.P.D. Detectives Ceretta and Logan arrive on the scene to face an angry group of demonstrators who are convinced the tragedy was no accident.

BURIED SECRETS . . .

Homeless activists blame the ruthless developer of the site. But as Ceretta and Logan dig deeper, they discover that the dead woman was once a wealthy socialite who knew the secrets of the city's power elite. Following a twisted trail of greed, violence and conspiracy, they uncover shocking evidence that points the finger of guilt at one of New York's most trusted citizens.

A CITY ON THE EDGE . . .

Now, pitted against a celebrated defense attorney and a storm of controversy that could tear the city apart, District Attorney Ben Stone fights to build an airtight case and deliver a cunning, cold-blooded killer to justice.

**Coming in June from
St. Martin's Paperbacks!**